"There's something I'm dying to find out..."

They stood face-to-face in the crowded restaurant, and when someone walked past, Layla was forced to step closer to Sam to make room. He watched her green eyes dilate in a telltale sign of arousal. "Oh? And what's that?" she asked lightly.

A slight upturning of her lush lips made his stomach crave something other than food. Continuing to play the game, he answered, "Whether or not you taste as good as you look."

Before she could respond, Sam closed the few inches separating his mouth from Layla's, giving her plenty of time to pull back. She didn't. In fact, she leaned forward.

Her mouth tasted like a juicy peach just begging to be devoured. He flicked his tongue out, licking the rim of her lips, then dipping it inside. He'd never tasted anything sweeter, hotter, more addictive...

Desire hit, strong and hard. And Sam suddenly realized just how *hungry* he really was....

Dear Reader,

Sugar 'n spice and everything…naughty. That description fits the three heroines in our KISS & TELL miniseries to a T. Especially Layla Hollister, no matter how much she'd like to have you believe otherwise. Especially when fellow physician and resident hottie Sam Lovejoy comes onto the scene.

In *Night Fever*, general practitioner Dr. Layla Hollister literally shivers whenever she hears plastic surgeon Dr. Sam Lovejoy's name. The truth is she would never have been attracted to him if she'd known who he was when they met. But she didn't know. And attracted? Well, that doesn't begin to cover how she feels about the notorious Dr. Lovejoy. The problem is once he catches on to her feverish condition, he relishes challenging her on all she's come to believe about life and love…and about hot, sticky sex!

We hope Layla and Sam's sizzling journey leaves you running for a cold shower! We'd love to hear what you think. Write to us at P.O. Box 12271, Toledo, OH 43612 (we'll respond with a signed bookplate, newsletter and bookmark), or visit us on the Web at www.BlazeAuthors.com and www.toricarrington.com for fun drawings.

Here's wishing you love, romance and hot reading!

Lori & Tony Karayianni
aka Tori Carrington

Books by Tori Carrington

NIGHT FEVER

Tori Carrington

TORONTO • NEW YORK • LONDON
AMSTERDAM • PARIS • SYDNEY • HAMBURG
STOCKHOLM • ATHENS • TOKYO • MILAN • MADRID
PRAGUE • WARSAW • BUDAPEST • AUCKLAND

This one's for the incomparable Kathryn Falk,
Lady of Barrow, the extraordinary Carol Stacy,
the gifted Giselle Hirtenfeld/Goldfeder
and the entire staff at *Romantic Times* BookCLUB.
You all are the stuff of which heroines are made!

ISBN 0-373-79109-7

NIGHT FEVER

1

A casting call went out for an actress with natural breasts to perform a love scene with heartthrob Ben Damon. Not a single candidate has stepped forward, leaving this reporter to wonder if there's a pair of natural breasts left in all of Tinseltown....

DOCTOR LAYLA HOLLISTER closed the latest edition of the gossip rag she'd picked up on her way to the restaurant and glanced at her own modest breasts. They were all but nonexistent beneath her high-necked white blouse. She resisted the urge to wave her hand and say, "Me! My breasts are natural!"

Not that it mattered. Of the nearly two million people in L.A. proper, not to mention the ten million in L.A. County, she was one of the ten percent not interested in an acting career. Not in a bit part in a commercial or music video. Not even in a starring role opposite one of the world's best-looking men. De nada. Add that she was also a third-generation Hollywood native whose family tree didn't include any actors and, well, she was even more of a rarity. She made a face, peeled off the piece of lime stuck to the side of her glass, and sipped on her club soda.

At any rate, the casting agents would get one look at her small bustline and probably laugh her out of the studio. Yes, they may be fishing for natural, but it was a pretty good bet they were looking for Halle Berry breasts and not her own boobs that essentially hadn't grown one iota since she was twelve and had bought her first training bra. Her well-endowed mother, Trudy, had told her she must have inherited them from her father's side of the family. Layla had thought it was God's idea of a cruel joke. At least until she was twenty and so busy with medical school she'd had little time to think about her breasts beyond the time it took to buy a new bra.

The paper rustled as she put it on the empty stool next to her. She glanced around the packed bar, wondering when her table would be ready. The restaurant she'd chosen had recently hit the trendy list, not because it was new, but rather because some star or another had stopped for a meal there and it had instantly become all the rage. She'd chosen it because it was close to home and she liked the food. So did Reilly, Mallory and Jack.

She sighed; just thinking of her three friends made her smile. She hadn't had many friends growing up. Okay, she'd had none—unless you counted Dirtbag Della who'd come to her house a couple of times back in second grade. Della had been the only person willing to hang out with the gangly geek in bottle-bottom glasses, at least until Della's mother had moved into a house where the shower worked and Dirtbag Della had suddenly qualified for Clique Three status. Then when Della had gotten a nose job at age eleven, she'd quickly moved up to Clique One and forgotten Layla existed altogether.

She found herself shrugging her shoulders even now, pretending not to care. And at twenty-seven, she really shouldn't. But she was only human and every now and again memories of her childhood in a town where looks were valued over everything else sometimes got to her.

She nudged her watch around her wrist. Where were Reilly, Mallory and Jack anyway? She was usually the one running late. As if on cue, her cell phone vibrated in the purse in her lap. She extracted the palm-size receiver, then answered when she saw the number was Reilly's.

"Can't make it, Lay. Sorry," her friend said without so much as a hello. "Last-minute order came in for three batches of Big Fat Greek Baklava and, well…you know."

Layla did know. The only thing worse than being an ugly kid in Hollywood was being a fat kid. And she sometimes thought that Reilly Chudowski— once known as Chubby Chuddy—had had it worse than Layla had. Reilly had long since taken off the weight, but she seemed determined to keep upsetting the status quo by opening a pastry shop called Sugar 'n' Spice smack-dab in the middle of healthy diet country. Surprisingly Reilly had turned a modest profit the first year. Now her goal was to corrupt the whole of L.A. with Sugar 'n' Spice.

"Give Mallory and Jack a kiss for me, will ya?" Reilly requested.

"We still on for next Saturday night?" Layla asked.

"Your place, right? Definitely still on. And I've got something special in mind just for the occasion." Reilly made kissing noises then rang off.

Well, that stank. Next Saturday was a good ten days away and she hadn't seen Reilly for at least as long. She'd hoped her day would improve with dinner. Instead it seemed to be taking an even sharper nosedive.

Layla slid her phone back into her purse, catching an envelope before it could fall to the floor. She flipped it over to read the return address. Her quarterly student loan statement. How long had it been since she'd actually paid any attention to her financial affairs? Her paychecks from both the Center and the clinic were deposited directly into her savings and checking accounts, and her loan payments automatically taken out. She had the same overhead every month—what with rent, utilities and car insurance—so there wasn't really much need to balance her accounts on a monthly basis. The problem was she was pretty sure a year or so had passed since she'd last sat down and gone over everything.

All her bank and loan statements sat on her foyer table unopened. Or she temporarily stuck them into her purse with the intention of opening them—which she never did.

She made a face. Wasn't that how people got into trouble? So she didn't like doing that sort of stuff. Who did, other than a boring accountant?

She slid her short thumbnail into the corner of the envelope and opened the statement. A quick glance told her that everything was going like a well-oiled machine. No flags to say that she'd missed a payment or that she was being penalized for anything. She stuffed the envelope back into her purse, figuring that's all she really needed to know.

"This seat taken?"

Layla blinked up into a pair of cappuccino-colored brown eyes a woman could easily fall into. A man who looked better than anything any menu could offer up was gesturing toward where she'd put the gossip magazine on the next stool. The seat was just about the only one in the place. Layla gestured at him. "It's all yours."

She covertly eyed the drop-dead-gorgeous guy; he had dirty blond hair and an even dirtier grin. Maybe her day had just gotten a whole lot better....

A MODEL. She had to be.

And Sam Lovejoy definitely liked models.

He grinned again at the tall, slender brunette as he took the stool next to her. He was at least twenty minutes early for dinner with the Trident Medical Center's senior board member. Hey, you couldn't be too careful in L.A. While the term "fashionably late" had likely come as a result of the rotten L.A. traffic, he prided himself on always being punctual. Even if that meant getting somewhere way too early.

Tonight it looked as though luck was on his side, though. As far as he could tell, the hottie next to him wasn't with anyone. And the way she kept sliding him glances told him she was open for any suggestion he might like to make.

He gave himself a mental thumbs-up and ordered a club soda.

"Twelve step?"

He raised his brows at the soft sound of her voice. She had one of those throaty voices that belonged in a smoky nightclub down on Sunset. "No, business dinner."

She smiled as she crossed her legs. Sam openly watched the movement, wishing her skirt was just a few inches shorter. "Not from L.A., are you?" she asked.

"That obvious?"

"Natives usually drink their way through meals, business or otherwise. In fact, they've been known to forego food altogether. It's what they call coping."

He handed her the paper he'd picked up from the stool. "Yours?"

She quickly accepted it. "My one vice." Her

smile was a knockout. "I'm obsessed with these things. Can't leave a store without picking one up." She tucked her thick dark hair behind her ear. "How long are you staying?"

"In L.A.? Oh, I don't know. I've been here for eight years and have no immediate plans for departure."

"Ah. In the business?"

"How do you mean?"

She gestured at the others around the bar, most trying to look important or as if they weren't scoping the place out for familiar famous faces. "Movie business."

"Oh, no. Not even close." Well, for all intents and purposes anyway. He didn't make movies.

She seemed to relax, and he chuckled.

"How about you?" he asked, plucking the lime from the glass and putting it on the napkin. Something she seemed to take note of. "Model, right?"

Her green eyes narrowed slightly. "Wrong."

"Then you should be."

While the comment was true, he got the distinct impression that she hadn't taken it as a compliment. He held up his hands. "Whoa. That sounded like one of the worst come-on lines on record, didn't it?"

"Mmm."

"Give me another chance?"

She stared at him for a long moment then cracked a smile. "To what? Embarrass yourself?"

"I deserved that."

She slowly sipped on her club soda through the tiny straw and stared thoughtfully ahead. "No, you didn't. I'm sorry. I'm having a really bad day today and it just got worse, and I guess you're the closest available target."

"Apology accepted."

She toyed with the napkin under her glass. "It's just that, well, one of my friends just cancelled out on me and my other two are late and..." She trailed off.

"And...?" he prompted, surprised to find he was waiting for what else she was going to say.

She waved her left hand—a hand devoid of jewelry. Her nails short and neat and clean. Most men might not notice something like that, but as a surgeon, Sam did. The expression "cleanliness is next to godliness" undoubtedly came from the medical profession.

"You don't want to hear this. Really you don't."

"You're right, I probably don't."

She stared at him.

"But since I still have..." he glanced at his watch "...at least a good fifteen minutes before my party arrives, listening to you sure beats watching the wallpaper fade."

Truth was, Sam was in an exceptionally good mood. His grandmother had always called him the Golden Boy, and when a college mate had overheard her calling him that, the tag had followed him throughout medical school and well into his career.

Not so much because of his looks, but because of his demeanor. While he experienced black moods like everyone else, the difference was he never let anyone know about them. But that didn't stop him from being interested in others.

"If I ask you a question, will you promise not to go cold on me?" he said when she fell silent.

"Depends on the question."

"Spoken like a true woman."

"You noticed."

His grin turned decidedly suggestive. Oh, yeah, he'd noticed. And then some.

Truth was he was highly attracted to the woman next to him. As far as first meetings went, he felt good about this one. She was elegantly gorgeous and obviously had more than a couple of marbles rolling around in her head. Most women he'd met over the past year would have immediately launched into a tale about a coffee enema gone awry when he asked about their dark mood. And while he still didn't know the source for her agitation, he'd bet it didn't have anything to do with coffee or enemas. And that was a refreshing change indeed.

"Who did your nose?"

WHO…did…her…nose…?

Layla absently rubbed the facial feature in question. It wasn't so bad that he had asked the question. It wasn't even bad if she *had* had her nose done. But the fact that an attractive nose—just like attractive breasts—instantly made other people think it was unnatural...well, rankled. The whole Hollywood bunch had made it virtually impossible for anyone outside the business to lead a normal life. She'd once joked that they should have some sort of government certification service that checked your body composition so that you had a certificate of authenticity that you could show to someone whenever they asked a stupid question like this.

Because no matter how she answered, the status of her nose would still be in question. After all, how many people who'd had cosmetic surgery admitted to it?

She opened her mouth and turned to give it to him good...but just looking into his handsome, inquisitive face robbed the air from her sails.

"Uh-oh. I've insulted you again, haven't I?" he asked good-naturedly. "Let me guess. The nose is yours."

"One hundred percent. And not in the 'I bought it so it's mine' way either."

"I guess I should be the one to apologize now."

She propped her elbow up on the bar and leaned her head against her hand. "No. It's not necessary. In this town it's a perfectly natural question. If anyone should be immune to L.A.-speak, it's me." She twisted her lips. "I don't know why I'm so touchy tonight. No, wait. Yes, I do. Because today I just found out I have a new boss."

"Ah. Someone I take it you don't like."

"Not a lick."

Layla picked at her napkin. Actually, she couldn't even say that, really. After all, she'd never met the guy. But his reputation had definitely preceded him. Known as the ultimate Chop Doc of L.A., he could nip, tuck, enlarge and siphon off whatever it was your li'l ole heart desired. From what she'd heard, wealthy clients and aspiring actresses alike lined up around the block for his services, and he had a waiting list as long as the Declaration of Independence. Except, in his case, the document would be entitled the Declaration of Dependence. Namely, dependence on a doctor to give you what nature hadn't.

Of course, it didn't help that it was rumored the doctor in question dated many of the patients he worked on. A new take on follow-up, she supposed. Nothing like getting a really good squeeze of the breasts you'd enlarged.

"I think that's why I'm so sensitive about anything related to plastic surgery tonight. I mean, I could have taken it if he was only another doctor at the Center, but he just signed on as senior staff administrator."

The man's hand knocked against the lip of the wood bar causing the club soda he held to splash out all over his wrist. He shook his hand and blotted his skin with a napkin. "Center?"

She nodded as she handed him her napkin. "The Trident Medical Center. Heard of it?"

"Santa Monica, right?"

"Right."

"You're a doctor?"

"A general practitioner, more specifically."

He motioned for the bartender to bring him another soda. "Not many of those around nowadays, are there?"

God, he was good-looking. He had breathtaking brown eyes that could put any actor's to shame. And that jaw...it came in second only to his mouth in items she most wanted to kiss in that one moment.

He looked at her pointedly, reminding her that he'd asked a question, albeit an indirect one. "No. There aren't many general practitioners around anymore. Everyone usually specializes in one branch of medicine or another. Me...well, I couldn't make up my mind." She smiled, liking the way he appeared to be listening to her. Not many men knew how to do that. "And there really wasn't any reason to do so. It turns out general practitioners are in high demand. Patients like to have one person to refer to instead of twenty."

"Mmm."

She pushed her elbow off the bar. "Now I feel as if I've said something to insult you."

His brows rose. Brows a shade darker than his dark blond hair. "Oh?"

"Yeah, you got awfully quiet. Change your mind about watching the wallpaper peel?"

"Fade," he corrected, then thanked the bartender when he got his drink. "And no," he said, looking at her, that suggestive glint returning to his eyes. In fact, the invitation in them seemed to go up a couple of notches. "Truth is…I'm very intrigued by what you said."

Intrigued?

Her purse vibrated in her lap again, reminding her that she was still waiting for Mallory and Jack.

"Pardon me," she said, fishing the wireless out. Yep, it was Jack. She turned slightly away. "Don't tell me you're canceling, too?"

She could hear traffic on Jack's end of the line. She instantly envisioned him driving his old Chevy with his windows rolled down. "Reilly cancelled?" he asked.

"How did…"

"I know because Mall just called from the 101. Engine trouble. I'm heading over to help her now."

Layla made a face and looked at her watch. "Sorry to hear that. I was really looking forward to tonight. Oh, well. It's busy here anyway. Maybe I'll just get a salad and head home. Give me a call later to let me know everything's all right?"

"Will do."

SAM WATCHED the sexy doc clap her phone closed and slip it back into her purse, feeling curiously as if he'd been whacked upside the head and sucker-punched at the same time. The first because he hadn't felt this strongly attracted to someone in a very long time. The second because, well, he barely knew her and she hated his guts. Not because of something he'd said. But rather because *he* was the new senior staff administrator at Trident.

Aw, hell. Talk about your small worlds.

Sam pretended to focus on something the guy on the other side of him was saying about the poor service, rather than on the doc's enticing legs. Meanwhile he considered his dilemma. Either he came clean now with the certainty that the attraction arcing between them would vanish like a flash of lightning. Or he continued to play dumb, pretending that she hadn't been specific about her information. Then he could try to take things on a bit with her—possibly even take her back to his house in the Hills—then hope that she would forgive him in the morning.

And he *would* have to face the music in the morning because if memory served him correctly, his first appointment tomorrow morning was with one Doctor Layla Hollister, the center's only female general practitioner. A getting-acquainted meeting that he'd prefer to conduct right now under present conditions…and without her knowing who he was.

"Your friends cancelled out, huh?" he asked.

"Yeah." She slung the strap of her purse over her shoulder, tucked the grocery-store rag under her arm and started to get up.

"Are you up for dinner with me, then?"

She looked at him, obviously tempted. "I thought

you had business to conduct.'' She tilted her head. ''I never asked what you did, did I?''

''No. And about the business dinner…I can always reschedule.'' He grinned at her, having made his decision not to reveal his identity. Not just yet. ''This is just too good an opportunity to pass up.''

She laughed. ''Unfortunately, I don't make a habit of picking up strange men in bars.''

''Shame.''

She nodded. ''Definitely a shame.'' She motioned to the waiter and placed an order for a salad to go. ''Hold my chair for me? I'm just going to go freshen up before I leave.''

''I think I can handle that.'' Good. At least this wasn't goodbye. Not yet…

He watched her head toward the restrooms at the back of the bar area. The material of her skirt hugged her high, firm bottom just so. Suddenly the temperature in the place seemed to jump at least twenty degrees. Sam tugged at his tie, emptied his soda, then got up. The bartender glanced at him as he slapped a twenty on the bar. ''Hold both seats, will you?''

Sam navigated through the sea of hot, young bodies crowding the restaurant, his mind on one hot, young body in particular. Oh, no, he didn't intend to let her get away that easily. He stopped outside the ladies' room and leaned against the wall. An opportunity was an opportunity. And he planned to take complete advantage of it.

The door to the restroom opened to let out a perky blonde. Sam rubbed his chin, then crossed his arms over his chest, ignoring her suggestive look.

The door opened again and Layla came out, stuffing something into her purse and appearing not to notice him. Sam lightly grasped her arm as she began to edge past him.

She blinked up into his eyes and a curious mixture of vanilla and lemon teased his nose. She smiled. A little welcoming, a little nervous. A slight upturning of the edges of her full mouth that made his stomach crave something other than food. "I thought you were holding my chair," she murmured, her gaze flicking over his features.

"Mmm. I was. But there was something I needed to find out first."

Someone walked by, forcing her to step closer to him to make room. He watched her swallow thickly and saw her green eyes dilate in a telltale sign of arousal. "Oh? And what's that?"

Heat surged through Sam's groin. "Whether or not you taste as good as you look."

He slowly closed the few inches separating his mouth from hers, giving her plenty of time to pull back. She didn't. In fact, she leaned forward. Sam made a low sound of satisfaction. He liked a woman who knew what she wanted and wasn't afraid of taking it.

And, oh boy, she tasted even *better* than she looked. She might smell like vanilla and lemon, but her mouth was a juicy, fleshy peach just begging to be devoured. He flicked his tongue out, licking the rim of her lips then dipping it inside. So hot, so sweet, so utterly intoxicating.

He felt her hand on his waist, her fingers splaying against the muscles there, boldly probing. Sam snaked his arm around her and tugged her closer yet, feeling every inch of her clothed body against his as he slanted his head and took a deeper taste of her. Damn, but she felt good. Need, sure and swift, swept over him as he slid his hand down her slender back toward the upper curve of her bottom.

Something between them vibrated. For a moment, Sam thought he was feeling the electricity generated by their mutual passion. But then he realized it was her cell phone.

He opened his eyes, surprised that he'd completely forgotten where they were.

He had to give Layla credit. Rather than jerking away from him or displaying surprise, she laughed softly and rested her forehead briefly against his. Then she cleared her throat. ''So what's the verdict?'' she asked.

''Hmm?'' Sam had to restrain himself from pulling her back to him when she stepped out of his arms. ''Oh. You definitely taste as good as you look. Better even.''

He heard that sultry laugh again as she dug into her purse and clicked open her cell phone. ''Hello?''

Hello was right. Hello, sunshine.

If only tomorrow's forecast didn't call for rain.

She snapped the cell closed. "I have an emergency at the clinic." She began to walk away, then hesitated. "It was nice meeting you…"

Nice didn't begin to cover it. "Same here." He took her hand and shook it, trying to ignore the heat that shot through his body at the contact. The dampness of her palm made him think of all things hot and wet. Now, how should he handle her subtle prompting for his name? "Let's just leave it at that, shall we?"

Her smile widened. "Why not?"

Why not, indeed? Sam thought, watching her walk away. He tried to keep a mental image of that beautiful smile, because he had a feeling that come tomorrow morning, he might never see it again.

2

THREE HOURS LATER Layla was stationed in the cramped room that served as the attending doctor's office in the San Rafael Free Clinic. She took a deep breath and dared to peek out into the waiting area, which, she saw thankfully, was nearly empty. Just a short time ago it had been overwhelmingly full.

She smoothed back a couple of stray strands of hair that had escaped from her ponytail. While the time she put in at the free clinic was rewarding, it was also exhausting. And often disheartening. So many people. So few doctors willing to help. It was especially disheartening when they'd just lost another attending physician and she'd been called away from a perfectly inviting encounter to fill the void.

Lupe Rodriguez, the clinic's long-standing head nurse, popped into the doorway and handed her a file. "Room two. Three-year-old with upper respiratory congestion. Room three, Ashanti's getting into position for her annual pap."

Layla watched an elderly woman tuck a tattered blanket more snuggly across a frail man's legs.

"Ola, Layla?"

"Hmm?" She glanced at the Hispanic woman waving a hand in front of her eyes.

"There's a thirty-something wealthy bachelor in room one looking for a hot night out."

Layla blinked several times then grimaced at Lupe. "That's not even funny."

Especially since the man she'd met at the restaurant bar earlier in the evening kept intruding on her thoughts. Sometimes it would just be a flash of his grin. Other times it would be his suggestive comments. But mostly it was the feel of his mouth sliding against hers. She'd be peering down a teenager's throat and remember the way he'd invited her to have dinner with him. Running her stethoscope across a patient's back and recall how wide his shoulders were. Definitely hot.

"How long's it been since you been out on a date?"

Layla took the patient file from Lupe and reviewed the preliminary information there. It wasn't that the question was intrusive, really. It was just that she'd been asking herself the same thing all night.

And the answer? Much too much time had passed since she'd sat across a dining table from someone who engaged her on every level. And the man in the bar had appealed to her physically and mentally.

"None of your business," she said to Lupe, smiling.

Lupe made a *tsk* sound. "That's what I thought. Too long."

Layla scratched her head. "Who's got time to date? I certainly don't."

Lupe crossed her arms over her ample chest. "I work here, what? Fifty, sometimes sixty hours a week for the past fifteen years and I not only dated, I got married, had five kids, and still manage to have a pretty good sex life, if you don't mind my saying so."

"I do mind. What you and your husband do behind closed doors is your business."

"And you?" Lupe teased. "What do you do behind closed doors, Dr. Hollister?"

"We already established that I don't date."

"What's a man got to do with it?"

Layla stared at her as if antennae had sprouted from her black, over-permed hair.

"Hmmph. That's what I thought." Lupe held the door open. "Let's go help someone who can be helped. You, Layla, are absolutely beyond hope."

Layla preceded her out of the room, trying to hide her exasperation. It was hard enough to successfully ignore the poor status of her love life without other people showing interest in it. Who else talked about her and her pathetic dating abilities? Oh, sure, she was busy. But as Lupe so adeptly pointed out, time or lack thereof had very little to do with a person's personal life.

Five kids? Did Lupe really have five kids?

She shook her head then strode to examining room three, opening the patient's file as she entered.

Ashanti. A nineteen-year-old who had more sex than ten women combined.

Or at least ten Laylas.

The young woman smiled at her from the examining table. "So, Doc, how they hanging?"

"Oh, they're hanging a little lower each day," she said automatically.

The problem was that there was no one around to notice...

THE FOLLOWING MORNING Sam repositioned the pothos plant his sister, Heather, had bought him, moving it first one way then another on top of a filing cabinet in his office near the window. But rather than being a gift in the true sense of the word, she'd done it to make a point. Simply that even though he was a doctor, he failed to look after himself. According to her, his days were focused way too much on work and not nearly enough on the small pleasures of life. No pets. No real hobbies—outside serial dating and an hour-long run in the morning. And the only reason he returned to the model of modern architecture in the depths of Hollywood Hills he called home, was to sleep. If pressed under threat of torture, he couldn't tell you the color of his bedroom walls, much less the makeup of the rest of the place.

"Come on, Porthos, buddy, you're not making me look good here," he said to the plant, reluctant to put his finger into the soil to see if it needed more water. Heather had given him the plant two months ago. And over that period it had gone from a lush, green plant to a dry, shriveled-up bunch of leaves. He sometimes wondered if it were still alive. No matter what he did, the plant looked worse. So he'd named it Porthos in honor of the musketeer who was popular among the ladies and had a mysterious suicide wish. Bringing Porthos to the office was a last-ditch effort to save the poor plant.

After picking up his empty coffee cup—another gag gift from his sister, it had a pair of gigantic breasts on the front, and a woman's arm for a handle—he made his way through the back door leading to what was called the center's personnel alley. Essentially it was where the doctors and other center employees could move around freely without being seen by patients. Its hub was a coffee-slash-lunchroom containing vending machines of microwaveable meals, your typical snack fare and three coffee machines, along with a cappuccino and an espresso machine. He put his cup under the tap for pure, full-octane coffee then glanced at his watch. Twenty minutes before one very delectable Doctor Layla Hollister found out he was the guy who had made her day so miserable yesterday.

"Hey, if it isn't Dr. Lovejoy," a male colleague came into the room from the opposite direction, navigating his way through the half-dozen other physicians already there. Bill Johnson was the center's top proctologist and got his kicks ribbing Sam. "Good thing you're not into proctology, huh, Sam?" he said as he put his cup in after Sam had removed his own. "Then again, I don't know. Dr. Lovejoy, proctologist. Has a ring to it, doesn't it?"

Susan Pollack, a pediatrician, nudged by Sam to get a packet of artificial sweetener. "I don't know. If your patients knew what some people said about you, Bill, they'd change physicians posthaste."

Sam lifted a brow. "What do they say?"

Susan smiled at him. "That, for Bill, proctology is 'been there, done that,'" she said. "You know, because of the, um, fact that he's gay."

Bill made a face. "I prefer *homosexual*. *Gay* makes me sound as though I should be performing in a musical on Broadway." He sipped his coffee. "And it's not like I hide my sexual preference. Not all homosexuals are queens."

"No, Bill, you definitely qualify as a king."

Sam laughed with good humor. "Okay, so is there any word on me yet?"

David Jansen, a cardiac surgeon, leaned back in a metal chair. "Nope. We figure your name is funny enough. Dr. Lovejoy, master of all things lovely and joyful."

"Or plastic," Susan made a face.

Sam chuckled. Having grown up with the name, he was used to the teasing—and to the long drawn-out way people had of saying his name, as if they were introducing the star of a porno flick. "Dr. Lovejoy in *Loves to Bring Women Joy.*"

Bill gestured toward Susan. "She's Suzie Q."

"David is Goliath," Susan shared.

Everyone went around the room quoting another doctor's nickname. Sam took a long drag from his coffee. "And Hollister? What's her nickname?"

The room fell silent for a heartbeat.

"You can guess at that one," Bill said, moving toward the door.

"Have you met her yet?" David asked.

Sam shook his head. "Not officially. But that'll be fixed in fifteen."

Susan gave him a level gaze. "Well, given her first name is Layla…"

"And she's drop-dead gorgeous," Bill added.

"You can only imagine what we say about her," David finished.

Sam supported his coffee cup with his other hand. "Fill me in."

Bill twisted his lips. "Well, there's 'Lay-no,' because she turns every guy in the place down flat. Present company excepted, of course."

David grinned. "There's 'needs-to-get-laid-now.'"

Sam nearly choked on his coffee.

"Then let's not forget 'Layl-aye-aye-aye,'" Bill added. "But of course that was a year or so ago."

"Oh?"

Susan made a face as she gathered up a chart from

the table. "If you believe the gossip mill, she went out with the sleaze down on two, Jim Colton, orthopedic surgeon, for a little while."

Sam considered that. "Ended badly?"

Susan opened the door. "Never should have begun. Colton's married," she told him in a conspiratorial whisper.

The room went quiet as the door closed behind her.

So Lively Layla had gotten burned by a doctor at the Center. That went a long ways toward explaining why she'd earned the later nicknames.

And made him even more intrigued by her.

"I take it none of you actually call her by any of these nicknames?" he asked, topping off his cup.

The five physicians looked at each other, then at him. "No," Bill said soberly. "We all like the family jewels right where they are, thank you very much."

Sam was thoughtful. "I'd do well to keep that in mind then, would I?"

He made his way back to his office, the comments moving around in his head. So Layla had a history at the center. Not unusual. Most doctors didn't have time to shop outside their immediate environs. He absently rubbed his neck. Judging by the little he'd gotten to know her the night before, however, he would have thought her smarter than to get involved with a married man. How long had the relationship lasted? A couple of dates? A month? Longer?

He made a mental note to check into this guy Colton. If he made a habit of preying on fellow physicians, he'd have to call him in for review.

He closed his office door and stood staring at the damn plant again. He'd half hoped the simple change in location would have made it perk right back up. His hopes were dashed. The thing looked even worse than it had five minutes ago.

"Pothos don't like direct sunlight," his medical assistant said as she came in from the other door. He glanced at Nancy Pullman, the woman he'd brought over with him from his private practice when he'd taken on the role of staff administrator.

"It's a plant. All plants like sunlight."

"Not pothos. It likes bright, diffused light, but not direct sunlight."

"We're in L.A. All light is diffused—by pollution."

She ignored his comment as she arranged files in his in-box, took items out of his out-box, then went through those items, putting half of them back on top of his desk. "You forgot to sign the follow-up release on the Golan woman. And I need you to rewrite your comments on the Fitzpatrick evaluation. I've warned you about your chicken scratches. If I can't read them, no one else can."

He grinned at her, not about to admit that he often had a hard time making out his own handwriting.

"What, do they teach that in How to Write Like a Doctor 101?" she asked, finally standing in one place long enough for him to get a look at her that didn't include a blur.

"Yeah, and I aced the course."

"Of course you did. Your sister says you aced all your courses."

"You sound disappointed."

"No. Just, after four years as your assistant I'm still looking for signs that you're human, that's all. Now are you going to move that plant, or shall I?"

He held up his hand. "I'll get it. Heather would never forgive me if she found out you helped me in any way whatsoever with this damn thing."

"Ah, Heather. That explains it. Another point she's trying to make, I take it?"

"Yeah. She said she'd wanted to get me a dog, but she thought a plant might be a better bet right now."

They both stared at the dying plant for a long moment, the comment settling in.

"Yeah, well, anyway." He put his coffee down on his desk then moved the sorry excuse for a plant from the window to his desk, just out of the sunlight.

Nancy held the documents to her chest. "Your nine o'clock is outside."

A good ten minutes early, Sam estimated. He liked punctuality in a woman.

Then he remembered that rather than looking forward to this meeting, Layla Hollister was dreading it.

"Well, we don't want to keep Dr. Hollister waiting now, do we?" He motioned toward Nancy while, at the same time, he signed the documents she indicated. "Send her in."

Two minutes later Sam forgot all about the conversation he'd had in the coffee room and remembered only how attracted he'd been to the woman the night before. Even in her plain white lab coat, she looked better than any woman had a right to. Last night she'd had her dark hair down. It was now in a French braid, exposing her nicely curved neck.

Well, at least the little of her neck that was visible above the white, chin-high collar.

Hadn't anyone told her this was L.A., not North Dakota, which was the only place it would be cold enough to wear such a shirt in October?

Layla's gasp told Sam he'd forgotten something else. Namely, that he'd purposely withheld his name from her the night before.

And, right now, seeing the look of horror on her face, he almost wished he had a different name.

EARTHQUAKE? Aftershock? Pre-shock? Layla fought to keep her balance as she matched the strikingly handsome face of the man standing in front of her with the face of the man who had haunted her dreams last night.

Her stomach bottomed out as she remembered just how very vivid those dreams had been. And just how many naughty things she'd had him do with that sexy mouth of his.

Unfortunately, her loss of equilibrium had little to do with the San Andreas Fault. Rather, it was shock due to the fact that this man had just reinforced her latest lesson in regards to men: they were all lying, cheating pigs who—if not for the temporary sexual relief they brought, or their procreative abilities—could line the bottom of the Pacific for all she cared.

"Dr. Hollister," he said, rounding his desk and reminding her just how very tall he was. She had to look up at him, something she wasn't used to since she was five foot eleven in heels. "Officially we meet."

He extended his hand. Layla curved hers against her leg to wipe the dampness away before stretching it out. "And last night would have been…"

"Unofficial."

"Ah. Yes. Of course." She tilted her head. "Which would make your not introducing yourself a simple omission rather than an out-and-out deception."

He feigned a wince. "Ouch." He seemed reluctant to take his hand back. And Layla realized with a jolt she was reluctant to have him take his hand back.

"Sam Lovejoy," he said casually, leaning against the edge of his desk. "And, yes, while it would probably be easier to pretend I didn't know who you were last night after you mentioned your…dislike of your new boss…" He let his words trail off. "Well, honesty is always the best policy, as they say."

"A little honesty probably would have gone a long way last night."

He rubbed his chin as if trying to erase his grin. It wasn't working. And neither was Layla's instinctive desire to respond with a smile.

"I probably would have told you at some point last night," he said. "You know, had you stuck around."

She crossed her arms. "Before or after we'd slept together?"

"Oh, after," he said without hesitation. "Definitely after." His gaze traversed her leisurely, making little shivers scoot all over her.

His cockiness, in addition to his bold honesty, made her feel hot all over. It was rare that a man could make Layla feel…small, somehow. No, not so much small, but vulnerable. If she threw up her hands right that minute and feigned a fainting spell, she imagined Sam Lovejoy would not only catch her, but would take complete advantage of the situation.

"Oh, I like that expression you're wearing right now. What are you thinking?" Sam asked.

Layla's smile widened. "None of your business."

"I'm your boss, in a manner of speaking, so everything that happens here at the Center is my business. Give."

Oh, he was good. "Well, let's just say that my thoughts were inappropriate, given our professional surroundings. Allow me to apologize for my insubordination.''

The gleam in his eyes told her he was impressed and intrigued by her daring comeback.

She held up her hand. ''Let me get one thing straight, Dr. Lovejoy.'' She cleared her throat, suddenly unable to say his name without shivering. Funny, just the day before she couldn't say his name without feeling disdain. ''If you haven't heard already, I made the mistake once before of becoming…intimately involved with a professional colleague.''

He nodded. ''I've heard.''

''Fast worker.''

''You have no idea.''

She cleared her throat again. ''Well, then, let me say point-blank that following that experience, I have no intention of getting involved with another colleague.''

His brows rose, nearly meeting the hair that swept across his forehead. ''Never?''

She smiled and shook her head. ''Never.''

Layla could hardly believe she was saying these words. She didn't play coy. She didn't indulge in verbal tit for tats. She didn't flirt the way she was doing with the handsome but very off-limits Dr. Lovejoy. This time her shiver nearly shook her from her sensible shoes.

And if ever there was proof that sometimes no meant yes, she'd just provided herself with exhibit one. Because if Sam put on the brakes and stopped flirting with her, she didn't know what she would do. She rested her hand against her neck, finding her skin burning. Well, she didn't know what she would do short of shoving him against the tall filing cabinets to her right and having her way with him.

"Point taken," Sam said, pushing off the desk and rounding it so he could sit down.

Two can play at this game, Sam thought as he tried to wipe the grin from his face and motioned for Layla to have a seat opposite him.

She seemed inordinately preoccupied with his filing cabinet. He wondered why as he watched her carefully sit down in the soft leather guest chair, her shapely knees together, her legs crossed at the ankles.

He couldn't recall a time when he'd enjoyed flirting with a woman more. Her initial disappointment at his deception pushed aside, she gave as good as she got. He fought the sudden urge to pull at his collar, knowing she'd be the same way in bed. Competitive. Bold. And so very, very naughty.

"It says here in your file that you volunteer at a free clinic," he launched into his official getting acquainted session.

"Ah, down to business," she said, finally meeting his gaze again. Was it him, or were her pupils a little large? "Actually, the clinic started paying me last year when the staff physician retired and moved back to St. Louis, and I essentially took over the role.''

He made the notation on a pad. ''This was the clinic you went to last night?''

She nodded. ''Yes.''

''How many hours do you put in a week?''

''Right now, since they're short of staff...about forty.''

He raised his brows. ''And you put in forty here.''

''That's right.''

Sam sat back in his chair. ''That doesn't leave much time for a personal life.''

The smile returned. ''No, it doesn't.''

He pretended to go through the file. ''Is there a husband or significant other around to complain?''

''No.''

He seemed to consider that, then he grinned at her suggestively. ''Good. Then there's no reason for you not to have that dinner with me tonight....''

3

"WE'RE BOTH consenting adults," Sam had said when Layla remained silent, more shocked than reticent. "You're attracted to me, I'm very definitely attracted to you. Let's see what impact dinner will have."

Three hours later back in her own office at the Trident Medical Center, Layla caught herself replaying the words. Her immediate reaction was no different now than it had been then. Her thighs dampened and her nipples strained against the front of her blouse as if seeking liberation. Or, more specifically, eagerly seeking the attention Sam Lovejoy appeared to want to give them.

"So don't leave me hanging. What did you say to him?" her friend Mallory's voice sounded impatient over the phone as she shouted over the noise of traffic. Sometimes it seemed as if Mallory's middle name was *impatient*. Layla was amazed by her rush through life in a take-no-prisoners way that left everyone else coughing in her dust.

Unfortunately, Mallory's driving—speeding, really—without directions usually left her facing a dead end.

A documentary producer by trade, a...what was she privately? Layla wondered. Chaos on wheels?

She smiled. No. Mallory was a great friend.

"I told him I have to work at the clinic tonight," she finally answered.

"Oh, Layla, you didn't!"

She leaned back in her chair, enjoying Mall's indignant reaction. "I most certainly did. Because it's the truth. Being short one doctor..."

"Screw the clinic," Mallory said then cursed up a blue streak. Good thing Layla also heard her car horn or she'd have thought Mallory was reaming her out. "You need to start looking after yourself for a change, Layla."

"Funny, that's what Sam said."

"Smart man, Sam. I like him already."

"Then you don't recognize his name."

"No. Why? Should I?"

"Remember that documentary you did, oh, about eighteen months ago?"

"The one on the elephant man's remains?"

"Close. The one on Hollywood's obsession with plastic surgery."

"Plastic surgery...Sam...oh my god! He's not *the* Dr. Lovejoy, is he?"

Even said in the elongated, condescending way Mallory uttered his name, Layla shivered. "The one and only."

"Kill him now. Before it's too late."

Layla laughed.

Mallory released a long breath. "Only you, Lay. Only you could be attracted to the one man in all of L.A. you shouldn't be attracted to."

"Who said I'm attracted to him?"

"You did, idiot. Just by mentioning him."

Layla made a face and toyed with the foil top of her yogurt container. Leave it to Mallory to sum things up within five seconds when she'd been trying to figure them out for the past three hours.

"So when *are* you guys going out?"

Layla raised her brows. "I didn't say we were."

"You didn't say you weren't, either. When?"

Layla sat up and tossed the half-eaten yogurt into the trash bin under her desk. "He invited me to his place for a late dinner tonight. You know, after I knock off at the clinic."

"Late-night nookie is more like it."

"Mall! I didn't say I was going. I just said that he offered the invite. He said something about it giving me an easy out if I needed it. You know, come, don't come. The ball's in my court." She coughed. "I, of course, turned him down."

"And he, of course, told you to think about it, that the invitation would remain open."

"How did…"

"A man of his stature is not known for giving up easily, Layla."

The sentence hung in the air before Layla's eyes in bright-blue neon letters. She heard the whoosh of traffic from the receiver and the sound of voices passing in the hall outside her office door, but all she could think about was what Mallory meant.

She rested her hand against her neck, noticing the heat there, the elevation of her pulse. As if it wasn't bad enough that Sam Lovejoy was a plastic surgeon, he was also rumored to be one of the biggest playboys on the Pacific coast.

He was also a great kisser. Just remembering his mouth against hers made her body tingle in response.

Mallory said, "Go."

"What?" Layla barely breathed the word.

"I said, go. I don't care how tired you are when you finish up at the clinic. You march right over to his place, strip out of your clothes before you're even through the door, and indulge in some meaningless, mindless sex." She sighed almost wistfully. "Lord knows, everyone else does."

"You don't."

"Yeah, well, that's because I'm probably one of the most uptight liberals this side of the equator." Layla heard the smile in her voice. "But I would want to go if I were in your shoes. I guess the question here is, do you want to go?"

Yes, she did. With every clench of her thighs. "No."

"Liar. Go. Then call me tomorrow with all the details."

"Now *that* I would never do."

"I know. Bummer."

A brief rap on her door, then the receptionist was motioning to her watch, letting her know her lunch break was over. Layla waved her acknowledgement. "Look, Mall, I've got to go. Good luck with the shoot this afternoon."

"I need more than luck—I need a miracle. But I'm still not letting you go until you tell me what you've decided."

Layla smiled. "Bye, Mall."

She slowly hung up the phone then sat there quietly for a long moment before moving on with her afternoon, no closer to a decision on the situation than she'd been at nine that morning.

It wasn't all that long ago that she'd vowed never to date a fellow physician again.

What was the saying? Once bitten, twice shy?

But she'd also gotten wiser. This time around she'd know the score going in. Sam wasn't married—she'd checked—but she knew he was a womanizer with a capital *W*. So if she did go tonight...if she did give herself over to this incredible desire...she'd do so knowing there could never be anything beyond great sex.

She swallowed hard. And there was no doubt in her mind that it would be great.

Another rap at her door. "Dr. Hollister?"

She shook herself out of her reverie and grabbed the chart in front of her. "I'm coming."

She caught herself up short, then shook her head and headed to see her next patient.

AT TEN-THIRTY that night, Sam opened the front
door to his sprawling house in Hollywood Hills and
heard the sound of the phone ringing. He waited for
his answering machine to pick up. When it didn't,
he strode toward the closest extension and picked
up the receiver, loosening his tie at the same time.

"What happened to your answering machine?" It
was his sister, Heather.

"Funny, I was just asking myself the same question." Carrying the cordless with him, he crossed
the large sunken living area, then punched the button
on the piece of black plastic. He had ninety-nine
messages. "I think it's full."

"I think it's broken."

"A possibility." He gave a wry smile. Leave it
to ever-practical Heather to point out the obvious.

"So what makes you call so late?" He shrugged
out of his suit jacket, tossed it across the steps, then
headed for the kitchen and grabbed a bottle of water
out of the refrigerator.

"Oh! Sorry. I guess I hadn't realized it was so
late. Is it really after ten already?"

"Brian working the night shift again?" Sam tried
to keep his voice casual, but somehow he was never
any good at it when it came to his sister's live-in
boyfriend. In the past three years they'd been together—two of them in the same house—Brian had
bounced around from job to job, the latest at a na-
tional shipping warehouse where he handled stock.

"Yes, as a matter of fact, he is," Heather said,

her tone telling him she wasn't buying the casual question either. "But that's not why I'm calling."

Sam downed half the contents of the water bottle then ran the back of his hand across his mouth. "Good, because if it was, I'd have to hang up on you."

"You wouldn't dare."

"No, I wouldn't." He screwed the cap back on the bottle and looked at his watch. It had been a long day filled with getting-acquainted meetings with staff personnel that hadn't been nearly as interesting as his meeting with Layla Hollister. Then he finished up with another dinner with the center director who, it appeared, was in the middle of a divorce and had nothing better to do with his time than schedule long dinner meetings with underlings who might prefer to be doing something else.

"Anyway, I was just thinking that it's been a while, you know, since you and I had some private time together."

Sam put the bottle on the counter and took off his tie. "I was just out for dinner with you and Brian the Sunday before last."

Oh, happy day. Brian had spent the whole time scowling into his beer can while he'd openly belittled the medical community at large and Sam more directly, and Heather had tried to smooth everything over. For her sake, Sam hadn't hauled off and given Brian a piece of his mind by way of a fist, but he probably would have had he stayed even five minutes longer. So he'd left as quickly as possible without looking back—which he wouldn't want to do anyway, considering the state of that place. The tract house was little more than a shack that his sister tried her best to make into a comfortable home.

He rubbed his face. "Do you need money?"

Heather laughed. "No, I don't need money. Thanks for asking. In fact, I'll have you know that I just started turning a profit."

"Making pigs?"

"Creating collectable porcelain pigs I sell on the Internet."

"Good." Sam massaged his forehead, feeling a headache coming on. With a great deal of assistance from him, his little sister had graduated from UCLA with honors. But after only one year in a promising public relations career, she'd met Brian and all her career ambitions had gone down the drain.

Now she was not only living with a pig, she was making them.

"No, I thought that you and I, you know, could go to our favorite place. Hang out for a while."

Their favorite place. Just the two of them. Sam grinned. That, he could definitely do. "Sure, name the time."

She did, three days from now, for lunch.

"Anyway, what are you doing home so early?"

"If you didn't expect me to be home, why did you call?"

"I expected to get your answering machine."

''You could have called my cell.''

''I never call your cell.''

''I know.'' He glanced at his watch. ''Interestingly enough, I have a date tonight.''

A pause. ''Have, as in, it has yet to begin?''

''Uh-huh. She's coming here after she gets off work.''

''And you talk about Brian working strange hours.''

''She's a doc and puts in time at a free clinic.''

''Same difference.''

Sam bit his tongue to stop himself from saying it wasn't.

''Is this serious? I mean, you never have anyone at the house.''

''I suggested a restaurant but she didn't bite. As for the serious part, this is our first date.''

''First date...at your house. Mmm. I was going to ask her name, but I won't, because I get the feeling her name won't come up again anyway after tomorrow.''

''Ouch.''

''Don't 'ouch' me, Sam. When are you going to stop all this dangerous playing around and get serious about someone?''

''Just as soon as I meet someone I want to get serious about. And what I'm doing is not dangerous. I have plenty of condoms.''

''You should hold stock in the company.''

''Actually, I do.''

She sighed heavily. "You know, one of these days I'm going to give up on you, big brother."

"No you won't."

"And what makes you think that?"

"Because you love me."

She laughed. "Yes, you big lug, I do."

Shortly thereafter Sam pressed the disconnect button on the phone then stood silently in the middle of his kitchen. Heather was ten years younger than him and was indirectly responsible for his having chosen to become a doctor. They were the only two children of Bruce and Louise Lovejoy of Toledo, Ohio, a quiet couple whose own parents before them had emigrated from England when they were young. But it had been Heather's being born with a cleft palate, and a local doctor's muck-up of the reconstructive surgery, that had given Sam the idea of becoming a doctor himself. A doctor that wouldn't make the same kind of mistakes his sister's doctor had.

He shook his head, wondering what had made his mind go back there. It had been a very long time since he'd thought about the genesis of his interest in the medical field. While Heather's scars were still visible because she refused to undergo further surgery, he'd spoken to her on the phone, not face-to-face, so seeing her scars hadn't been the reason for his recollections.

He glanced at his watch again. Layla should be

closing the clinic doors right about now. Of course, that didn't mean she would be heading this way.

He grinned. Nor did it mean that she wouldn't be.

He placed a call to a local restaurant and ordered up dinner for two to be delivered in fifteen, then headed for his bedroom and the shower beyond, not about to make it easy for her to refuse him if she did make the trip all the way out to his place.

OKAY, so Mallory was right. She did want to go to Sam's place. More than that, she was sitting in her car outside his house, hesitant about pulling into the driveway of the sloping ranch-style dwelling that could have held five of her cramped apartment.

Of course, she doubted Sam Lovejoy had the student loan debt that she had, either. His house alone stood testament to the fact. Never mind the sleek black Jaguar parked in front of the door.

God, he was home.

She wiped her damp palms on her skirt, not realizing until that moment that she'd secretly hoped he wouldn't be there. Then she could have placed the blame for their not seeing each other on him.

But he was home and she was there and it would be stupid for her to do anything else but go in. Maybe have a cup of coffee or water or something. Then say something about an early morning and hightail it out of there if she felt the least bit uneasy.

She made a face, backed up then pulled her ten-year-old Pontiac behind his sports car. Who was she

kidding? She didn't want to hightail it out of anywhere. She wanted to see if his mouth was capable
of doing all the things she'd dreamed about last
night. And, let's face it, it had been a good long
time since she'd had an orgasm that required somebody else being in the room. Much too long.

And if a little voice told her that this might not
be such a good idea, sleeping with a fellow doctor,
much less a boss of sorts, she ignored it. While Sam
Lovejoy might be staff administrator, he was also a
man. And while she couldn't really say she knew
him all that well, she got the distinct impression that
any indiscretions would be kept between the two of
them. Unlike what had passed between her and Jim
Colton. It seemed the entire Center knew that she'd
had an affair with a married man. The only people
who hadn't had a clue, it appeared, were her…and
his wife.

"Turn off the car, Layla," she quietly ordered
herself.

She did, then forced herself to climb out. The
lawn on either side of the drive was nicely land-
scaped. Flowers blooming everywhere. But that
didn't mean anything. All the houses out this way
had professional landscapers. It didn't mean that…

What? That Sam was married?

She stretched her neck. No, she'd been extra careful this time out. If there was one thing she was
absolutely positive of, it was that Dr. Lovejoy
wasn't married.

Of course, that didn't mean he wasn't in or hadn't very recently been in a serious relationship on the verge of marriage.

"Oh, for God's sake, Layla, get over yourself. Just because you've been burned once doesn't mean you'll be burned again."

There were no guarantees that she wouldn't be, either, she reminded herself.

She walked to the door, straightened her skirt, then raised her hand to knock.

"It doesn't matter anyway. You're just here for the sex."

The door opened midway through her comment to herself and Sam stood there in all his handsome glory, a mile-wide grin on his striking face. "Did I hear somebody say 'sex'?"

4

Oh, yeah, sex was definitely what was on Sam's mind. Hot, sweaty, monkey sex with one very delectable looking Dr. Layla Hollister.

And he wanted it *now*.

In fact, given his immediate and acute reaction, you'd have thought she'd shown up at his door wearing a see-through teddy rather than the same skirt and blouse she'd had on this morning. It was then he noticed her clothes looked a bit rumpled. Also, strands of her dark hair had sprung from her once neat French braid, and whatever makeup she'd had on was long gone. But rather than make her unattractive, the effect was…phenomenally appealing. Her green eyes were huge, her lips sexily kissable, her hair tousled in a way that made him think of smooth sheets and squeaky bedsprings.

And Sam wanted to forgo all pleasantries, throw her over one shoulder and take her to his cave so he could have his wicked, wicked way with her.

She smiled slightly. "That's it. I'm convinced of it. All men are born with *sex* branded across their cerebral cortexes."

Sam opened the door farther. "Mmm. I wasn't

the one who said the word.'' He watched her enter hesitantly, her gaze taking in everything she could see. ''It's the rest of the sentence I'm curious about.''

''I bet. Do you mind?'' She rested her hand on his shoulder to steady herself as she slipped out of her low-heeled shoes. He waited to see if she had any other article of clothing in mind next, but unfortunately she stopped there.

''You know, as your doctor, I have to tell you those shoes don't do anything for your posture when you're on your feet all day.''

''So now you're my doctor?''

He shrugged. ''No. I just play one at work. And it looks as though you need one.''

She laughed quietly. ''As far as compliments go, Dr. Lovejoy—'' Was it him or had she just shuddered? ''—that one leaves a lot to be desired.''

Desired...

Oh, that was a word that nicely described what she was for him. He desired her—in his house, at this late hour, looking like she needed a sack session as badly as he did.

She released her hold on him, swept her shoes to the left of the doorway, then walked a little farther into the room.

Sam's gaze skimmed up the back of her long, long legs, to the waist of her impossibly long skirt, and up to where wisps of hair teased the back of her collar. "How long has it been since someone has looked after you?"

She slanted a gaze over her shoulder, wariness backlighting her eyes. "And the compliments only get better."

He chuckled, suddenly glad he'd put on a polo shirt and jeans. If he had answered the door buck-naked, as he had wanted to, she likely would have run in the other direction.

Not to mention that he might have ended up scarring the food-delivery guy for life.

Somehow he wouldn't have guessed that the lovely Layla would have casual sex problems. The way she flirted indicated she was up for anything anytime. But the way she seemed so guarded now...

Sam considered her.

Yes, this Layla would take a little bit of work. But, oh, what a job it would be. He had little doubt that once he stroked her in just the right way, she'd purr like a sex kitten and fulfill all of his fantasies.

He hiked a brow. All of them? Now that was a concept. He usually liked different women for different reasons.

But Layla...

Layla he found he wanted every which way he could have her.

"I ordered some delivery. It's in the oven keeping warm. Are you hungry?" She shook her head. He'd suspected that would be her answer. He'd have to take things a little slower yet. "When's the last time you had a bath?"

She turned her head so he could see her profile. "Are you saying I'm unclean now?"

He cocked a grin. "No, I'm saying you look like you could use a soak."

Her head bent toward her chest. "I think I was four the last time I had a bath."

"That long?"

She rubbed the outer part of her left arm with her opposite hand. "Pretty much. The place I live in now only has room for a shower."

Two steps brought Sam near enough to smell her. The subtle scent of vanilla teased his nose along with that lemony tang he'd smelled last night at the bar. He realized the second scent must be her hair.

He lightly touched her shoulders. She jumped slightly, apparently unaware he was so close, but didn't protest when he steered her toward the long counter separating the living room from the kitchen. The coiled tension in her muscles nearly singed his palms.

Then again, that could be the result of a sexual tension so strong that it had her on fire. The question was, would it be so overpowering he'd get burned?

"Wine. Red. How about we start with that?"

She allowed him to sit her down on a wood bar stool, but he suspected that was more because she wasn't up to fighting him than because of any real desire to sit. She glanced at her watch. "You know, I shouldn't even be here. We've both got..."

"Shh," he said, noticing that her hand was trembling slightly. "A little wine never hurt anybody."

Then a bath. Yes, definitely a bath. He could already see her stretched out in his whirlpool, bubbles foaming around her sexy shoulders.

He opened the pantry door, then the refrigerator and looked around on top of the counter before he remembered he had one of those wine-cooler things under the cabinet she sat at. He chose a bottle from a selection someone else had stocked, then turned to find a corkscrew, all the while aware of her watching him and looking around the open living area, her eyes growing narrower.

"Got it," he said, finally locating a newfangled corkscrew from a drawer filled with cooking accessories.

He poured a portion into a glass he blew into first and then he tried to hand it to her. But she was holding up her hand and getting up from the stool.

"Whoa. What's going on here?"

Sam took the wine back, holding the glass to his chest. "How do you mean?"

"Well, for starters, the pink and red pillows on your sofa? No man would ever pick those out." She frowned. "At least no man interested in women."

He looked at the decorative pillows she was referring to, admitting she had a point. He certainly would never have chosen them.

She was gesturing with her hand as she backed up toward the door. "You didn't even know you had a wine cooler, for God's sake. And the corkscrew..." Her neck snapped straight. "Only a married man doesn't know where everything is in his own house."

Sam grimaced, not liking where this was heading. "Or a man who just recently moved into a house, doesn't spend a whole helluva lot of time in it, had a professional see to the decorating and has a housekeeper who comes in a couple of hours in the morning and stocks everything when he's not here."

The wariness hadn't left her eyes, but at least she'd stopped moving backward.

He casually rounded the counter and came to stand in front of her.

She brushed the loose strands of her dark hair back from her face. "I'm...sorry. It's just..."

He held out the glass again. "Hey, no apologies necessary. More people should be so cautious."

She accepted the glass and drank slowly from it.

"Speaking of caution, did you bring condoms?"

LAYLA nearly spewed the mellow Merlot all over the front of his white polo shirt.

Oh, that would be cute. She fingered her lips as she took him in. Had she ever met a man as charmingly disarming as Sam? One minute he seemed to be insulting her. The next he made a comment so bawdily sexy and funny that she wanted to laugh and strip her clothes off at the same time.

Never mind that his grin did sizzling things to her nerve endings.

He slid his hands into his jeans pockets then shrugged. "'Cause, you know, if you didn't, I don't want you to be shocked that I have them on hand."

Not only was he not exasperated by her moronic behavior, he was going out of his way to help her relax. Not many men were capable of doing that. Then again, she was coming to see that Sam wasn't like many other men.

She glanced over the living room again, noting that it did have that new, unlived-in feeling about it. Even the magazines on the coffee table looked untouched. And the plants artfully placed around the room were all silk.

"You know," Sam was saying, "You should feel privileged. I don't invite many women back to my place. And on the first date...well, virtually unheard of."

Layla smiled widely. "Privileged, huh?"

"Mmm. Yeah, some women get weird when you let them through the door of your house. You're not going to get weird on me, are you, Dr. Hollister?"

"Depends on your definition of weird."

"You know, put your toothbrush in the holder next to mine, put your tampons next to my shaving cream. That kind of thing."

He had such a delicious sense of humor. "Nah. I usually save that for the second date."

"Then we'll have to make sure that second date is at your place, then."

"Providing we both survive the first."

"Very right."

They stood like that for a long moment, neither of them saying anything, both of them sizing up the other. Then Sam took the glass from her hand and murmured. "Well, then, let's get started, shall we?"

One moment Layla was watching him put the wineglass on a low table nearby, the next she gasped as his fingers slid over her cheekbones then to the back of her hair. He released the clip there, then languorously fingered the strands free.

He tilted his head one way, then the other, his deep-brown eyes almost glowing with need, then, finally, he was kissing her.

Oh, yes, Layla thought, giving herself over to the feel, the taste of him. Now she remembered why she'd driven the half hour to his house in the middle of the night....

THIS was definitely much more like it.

Sam had always enjoyed a challenge. But usually they came in the form of a predatory female who had read somewhere that playing hard to get caught a man's attention. He usually agreed and rose to the occasion in more ways than one.

But Layla...

There wasn't one thing about her that was manipulative, and to her, none of this was a game. He wasn't a pawn to be positioned, conquered or toyed with. She clearly grappled with issues he couldn't hope to understand that kept her wary and at arm's length.

She also very clearly wanted him in a way that made his libido answer loudly in response.

Damn, but she was a good kisser. Closed-mouthed, openmouthed, nibbling, licking, her lips moved in concert and in opposition to his, igniting in him a hunger that made him want to claim her in all ways. Her hands fumbled with the hem of his shirt then she was pushing her palms up the expanse of his waist to press against his nipples, her short nails lightly raking his skin. Her moves were bold and daring, in sharp contrast to her cautious wariness only a moment ago.

"The…bedroom…is…" He was going to say down the hall, but when her fingers dove for the button to his jeans, his sentence snapped in half along with his ability to hold on to a coherent thought. Ragged breathing filled his ears. His blood surged through his veins as if on a very important mission. And his hard-on pulsed as he pressed it against her soft flesh through their clothes.

He turned her so they could stumble down the two steps to the rich burgundy leather sofa, at the same time lifting his arms to allow her to take off his shirt. Then he went to work on her godforsaken, multibuttoned blouse.

"Torture contraption," he muttered, kissing her even as he fought to monitor his progress with the buttons.

She moved his hands out of the way and made quick work of them, allowing the lightweight material to float down her arms and to the floor while he appreciated the ivory silk chemise she had on underneath. Given the nature of his work, he'd seen countless breasts. Even debated with colleagues about what went into making the perfect breast. But in this one moment the prospect of seeing Layla's bare breasts drove him mad with excitement.

And, of course, her marauding hands weren't hurting matters either.

Open went his fly and inside the band of his sports boxers went her fingers, stroking the length of him in a way that made it very hard to be in his own skin.

"You're killing me here, Layla," he murmured, finding the catch to her skirt. He undid it, and she kicked it away, revealing a pair of matching ivory and lace underwear that hugged her in all the right places.

He trapped her head in his hands as he kissed her deeply, holding her there until they both were forced to pull away for air.

"Those...condoms," she whispered. "Do you have any on you?"

Sam honestly couldn't think straight. "Pockets..."

Her cheeks where flushed. "Which one?"

"All of them."

Her green eyes twinkled with amusement as she took a condom from his front right pocket, then shoved his jeans down around his ankles. She opened the packet with her teeth, her gaze glued to the part of him she had revealed and was about to sheath.

"Mmm." She blinked her hooded eyes to look into his. "For me?"

"Every last inch," he said, taking the latex from her fingers and rolling it down over his turgid flesh.

She collapsed to the couch and he grasped her hips, turning her until her firm rump was in the air.

He stood behind her, admiring the sight before him. Good God, but she had an incredible ass. The kind a guy wanted to take a bite out of. He smoothed his hand down her back, from the cool silk of her chemise to the hot skin peeking from beneath it. He pressed on her lower spine so that her bottom came up even farther off the edge of the couch.

Sam nearly groaned, watching as her silk undies strained against her swollen womanhood, a damp circle showing her want of him even as she unconsciously strained backward, looking for contact.

He helped her shimmy from her underpants, revealing a neatly trimmed but fully intact triangle of hair with tight springy curls. Not a sight a guy in

L.A. got to see every day. Brazilian bikini waxes were all the rage nowadays. Though he'd die to see Layla that way too....

"Sam..." she breathed his name on a ragged breath.

He realized he was dropping the ball on his end, so entranced was he with the view. He curved a finger and ran it the length of her dripping crevice, her clit engorged and trembling, her flesh swollen and waiting. He pulled her until her hips were even with the dark leather, his fingers indenting the pale skin of her bottom. He inched his thumbs nearer her fissure then drew the concealing skin back, baring her rose-colored folds to his gaze.

Her soft moan told of her building passion. But as much as he wanted to drive into her to the hilt, he wanted something else more in that one moment. He leaned over and drew his tongue the length of her womanhood then fastened his lips around her hooded flesh and sucked.

Layla instantly climaxed, her soft cry loud in the quiet room. Her body jerked and writhed and convulsed as he continued to suckle. Then just when she was about to go still again, he took away his mouth and filled her with his throbbing erection.

Sam had to grit his teeth against the spiraling need to come right then. He held onto her hips tightly and stilled himself, trying to concentrate on something other than the overwhelming sensation washing over him. Then, finally, he moved. He slid in...and out.

In…and out. Watching, entranced, as her swollen flesh accepted him, then reluctantly allowed him to retreat, her moans growing lower, and longer, her fingers digging into the soft leather of the couch, her back arched as she strained against him.

Flames licked around the edges of Sam's tenuous control. He tensed his muscles to ward off his coming climax. He didn't want this exquisite pleasure to end yet. Wanted to keep Layla right where she was for as long as possible. Feel her hot, slick flesh contract against his. Listen to her soft sounds. Watch her hips buck and seek and grind.

He thrust in to the hilt, holding her tightly against him. At that moment, her soft muscles convulsed violently around his hard-on, rendering him helpless to stop the thundering sensations from careening him over the edge and launching him into the bright-red stratosphere.

What seemed like a long time later, he lay against her back, his fingers smoothing her hair away from her damp face, his erection twitching inside her as she trembled beneath him.

Then she made a sound that sounded suspiciously like a laugh. He shifted slightly to see that, yes, indeed it was.

Dr. Layla Hollister, the woman he had just enjoyed incredible sex with, was softly laughing.

"Was it something I did?" he asked quietly.

She reached back, her fingers grasping his hips. "Oh, yeah. It was definitely something you did."

"Care to share?"

"No."

Sam grinned then burrowed his nose into her lemony-smelling hair.

"I mean, no, beyond saying thank you, that is."

He closed his eyes, enjoying the moment. "Ah, a good one, huh?"

"Mmm. *Good* doesn't begin to cover it."

He peeled himself from her feverish body, withdrew, then turned her over so that her knees were on either side of his hips. Her green eyes twinkled suggestively, her mouth was curved into a smile as she watched him discard the old condom then don a fresh one.

"Good, because we've only just begun."

She opened her mouth, probably to say another saucy remark, but he didn't give her a chance as he filled her from the front....

5

_____

"HERE ARE the graphs you asked me to work up." Nancy dropped a file on top of the chart Sam was reading. He reared back in his chair with a squeak.

"You know, you could knock every once in a while. Let a body know he's about to be ambushed."

Nancy didn't even blink as she moved his plant from one corner of his desk to the other then stared at the puddle left behind. "You're drowning the sorry thing."

"Too wet. Too dry." He stared at the plant that had become the bane of his existence lately. When Heather had initially given it to him, he'd thought, "Hey, no problem. It's a plant. How difficult can it be?" He'd quickly found out just how hard it was, and it was growing into an obsession with him, his need to see that this plant not only survived, but thrived. "That thing's going to be the death of me."

Nancy looked at him over the rims of her reading glasses. "Oh, somebody's grumpy this morning. What, late night?"

Sam grinned then opened his mouth.

Nancy held up her hand. "Spare me the details."

She opened a drawer, took out a pile of paper napkins, then cleaned up the mess on the desk before plucking the files out of his out basket. "Your one o'clock cancelled. Maybe you can fit in a nap."

Sam stared at the graphs in front of him. "Thanks. Maybe I will." He glanced at the leather couch up against the opposite wall. He and that couch had become very well acquainted over the years. Of course, he hadn't used it yet since signing on at the Trident Medical Center. Mostly because it was a new gig for him and the challenge allowed him no breaks. Also he'd promised at least a ten percent increase in staff productivity and income within the first six months.

He scratched his head. Of course, that had been before he'd seen that the staff at the Center already worked harder than most staffs. And that there was very little for him to work with.

"Are these accurate?" he asked, waving the top graph at Nancy who was at the filing cabinets fingering through the top drawer.

She stared at him, closed the drawer, then left the office.

"Of course they're accurate. Nancy did them," he said absently, settling in to examine the papers.

He rubbed his temples as he followed the different colored bars, which only verified what he already knew: that the next six months were going to be hard. One lower bar caught his eye and he squinted at it, following it over to the name to the left. If this was right, then Dr. Layla Hollister's patient load was remarkably below that of the other staff physicians. He thumbed through the other graphs, finding that the others put in ten-hour days while Layla put in eight-hour days, knocking off promptly at five each evening. That alone would explain a twenty percent difference. He glanced at the first graph again, estimating that's about where things stood.

Of course, he knew why. Because she worked at the free clinic down on Sunset in the evenings.

He knew that as her lover he'd prefer to overlook it, but as staff administrator...well, he'd have to talk to her about it.

Lover...

He leaned back in his chair again and entwined his fingers over his stomach. Oh, yeah. *Lover* very definitely described what he was feeling like. Last night...last night had surpassed anything he'd done in a long, long time. She'd been insatiable. Hell, he'd been insatiable. The more he had of her, the more he'd wanted her.

Even now, merely thinking about her brought about a reaction that wasn't all that appropriate, given his present surroundings.

He stretched his hands behind his neck and leaned his head back against them, unable to wipe the grin from his face. Layla had been incredible. More responsive than any woman he'd been with for a long, long time. They'd connected in a way that he knew was rare. How did he know that? Well, because if he reviewed his relationships over the past ten years, he and Layla had done in one night what usually took at least a month to get around to with other women. *If* those other women made it that long. And it wasn't because Layla was submissive or he'd been on Viagra. Rather what had happened between them came about as a result of chemistry and mutual desire. They'd matched in every way.

He glanced at his watch. The problem was he wouldn't be able to further explore the new phenomenon for at least another ten hours, about the time she knocked off from work at the clinic.

They hadn't arranged to meet again. But when they'd parted this morning, both of them had known they would.

He yawned in a leisurely way that made him grin even wider. But if he hoped to make it tonight, he'd definitely have to squeeze in a power nap. He closed his eyes, letting images of Layla's delectable body and what she'd done with it slide through his mind.

The next thing he became aware of was Nancy knocking his feet from his desk.

''Wipe the drool from your chin, Doctor,'' she said in that way she had while not looking at him. ''Your two o'clock is waiting in the next room.''

Two o'clock.

Sam got up and headed for the washroom. Only nine more hours to go...

''CALL ME. It doesn't matter how late it is. I don't get off until ten anyway.''

Layla listened to the answering-machine message her mother had left as she let her purse slide off her shoulder and onto the apartment floor, then shrugged out of her jacket. She glanced at her watch. Past eleven. But the issue really wasn't the time. Rather she didn't know if she had the energy to listen to her mother complain about how long it had been since Layla's last visit...or how much time had passed since her last phone call.

Layla rubbed the wrinkle between her brows. How long had it been? A week? Two?

"Elizabeth, this is your father."

Of course it was. Her father was the only one who called her by her middle name instead of her first. She suddenly felt even more tired.

"Sharon and I are extending an invitation to dinner next Sunday. Casual dress. Unless I hear otherwise, we'll expect you at one o'clock."

Great. That's all she needed. A five-course dinner at her father's monstrous estate to make her feel even more inadequate than she felt already.

"Um, hi."

Shivers ran up and down Layla's back at the beginning of the third message. *Sam.*

"Ten minutes," he said simply. "That's all I need to get there."

He then left her his cell number.

She pushed the replay button and listened again. Then one more time, leaning against the wall next to the telephone stand as she did so.

Ten minutes…

Suddenly Layla no longer felt tired but exhilarated. He'd called. He'd not only called, but he wanted to see her again.

The sound of her thick swallow sounded loud in the small apartment. She reached for the receiver, then noticed the way her hand shook and pulled it back.

"Get a grip, Lay. You're not in high school anymore."

She plucked up her purse and put it in the closet along with her suit jacket then stepped out of her shoes and picked them up to take into her bedroom with her. Fifteen minutes later she had showered, tidied up, and rather than craving the sleep she'd yearned for only a half hour ago, now all she craved was Sam.

Did she dare? She'd gotten no more than two hours sleep last night. And if she let him inside her door now…well, sleep would pretty much be out of the question tonight.

She absently smoothed back her damp hair, wondering how long a person could go without a solid eight hours. What was she talking about? She hadn't had a solid eight hours sleep since interning at UCLA Medical Center six years ago, signing on at Trident five years ago, then adding her work at the clinic three years ago. Essentially, she had caffeine for blood.

But right now she'd settle for four hours sleep.

She picked up the cordless receiver and dialed the number Sam had left, told him she'd be ready in fifteen, then hurried to her bedroom to dry her hair and change her sheets.

LAYLA'S art-deco apartment in Wilshire was cramped but cozy.

Sam stood in the middle of Layla's living room and took everything in. His walk-in closet boasted more square footage than her entire apartment. But it had a pretty view of a courtyard with a fountain, and she'd packed more character in the small space than there was in all the rooms in his house combined. Pink-and-white striped fabrics competed with muted florals. And it was obvious she didn't share his black thumb because plants flourished everywhere she could fit one. Candles of different sizes and shapes all flickered, filling the room with a warm, intimate glow.

Layla cleared her throat next to him. "Student loans."

"Hmm?"

"The reason I'm still living here instead of a bigger place."

"Ah," Sam said, remembering that period of his life too well. Life was all fun and games until you interned and realized how much debt you'd racked up.

He turned to offer up the food he'd brought. "Chinese."

Her smile would have put a thousand-watt bulb to shame.

"I figured you probably hadn't eaten. And I could sure use some protein." He grinned at her suggestively. "The best thing about Chinese is it's self-contained. No dishes to wash." He liked the way her plain white T-shirt and jeans fit her. "That is, if you know how to use chopsticks."

She accepted the bag. "Oh, I think I can manage. Beer?"

"Caffeine-free soda?"

She hiked a brow.

"Don't know if the system can handle alcohol right now."

"Two sodas coming up."

Within minutes she'd repositioned medical journals, gossip magazines and candles around the low coffee table and set up a virtual buffet of Chinese take-out cartons.

"You must really be hungry," she noted as she accepted the chopsticks he handed her.

"Mmm," he responded idly as his gaze skimmed the tempting curve of her neck where she had her hair pulled back in a ponytail.

She crossed her legs on the sofa next to him, the only place to sit unless you counted the old wooden rocker off to the side of the room. "So how was your day?" she asked, manipulating the sticks to take some rice from one carton then dip it into the sauce from another.

Such a simple question really. One people asked each other all the time, like "How are you?" But considering he'd spent the entire time obsessed with when he'd get to see her next, the question emerged anything but normal.

"Oh, I don't know. Your typical everyday workday, I guess. Yours?"

She laughed quietly. "I spent every spare moment thinking about last night."

Not so different from his day except he'd been thinking about tonight. "Ah."

"Yeah, ah." Her green eyes sparkled as she took a long sip of canned soda.

"You?" he motioned with his sticks toward a framed photograph on the end table.

The sparkle went out of her eyes. "Yes."

He put a potsticker into his mouth, stabbed his chopsticks into a rice carton, then picked up the simple frame. In a professionally done portrait, a girl of about twelve or so knelt next to a leather armchair in which an older man sat. "Your dad?"

She nodded, seeming to pay inordinate attention to the food as she decided what to eat next. "I was fifteen and I had just met my father the month before."

Fifteen? She was fifteen in the picture? He squinted at the expensive portrait, examining the slender girl she'd been. It could have been the thick glasses she was wearing. Or the fall of her hair, but she didn't look any older than twelve in the shot.

Then again, it might also be the vulnerable expression she wore...

At fifteen he'd tried his best to look like David Hasselhoff, chiseled pecs and all, and wouldn't have been caught dead with his nose in a book. Fifteen-year-old Layla looked like her pale nose had spent far too much time caught in the binding.

"Adopted?" he asked, putting the frame back down.

"Excuse me?"

"I asked if you were adopted? You know, since you said you'd just met your dad for the first time."

"No." She shifted as if trying to find a more comfortable position, tucking her legs off to the side instead of sitting with them crossed. She didn't say anything for a long moment, then, "It's a long story."

He gestured toward the food. "Well, considering all we have to eat, I'd say it should give us enough time to listen to an unabridged audio version of the Old Testament."

"That would probably be more interesting."

"I doubt it," he said. "I don't know the people in the holy book personally. And when I say personally I mean—"

She groaned. "If you say 'in the biblical sense' I'm going to bean you with my chopsticks."

"I was going to say 'and when I say personally I mean very personally,'" he lied.

"I bet."

"And I'm waiting."

Again that reluctant look. She'd apparently decided what she liked best out of the selections and had picked up a carton. Now she put it back on the table. "My parents had a fling when they were at university." She took a sip of soda, not really looking at him as she spoke. "Or, rather, my father was at UCLA, my mother worked in a nearby sports bar. Although I guess back then it wasn't really a sports bar, per se, but a bar bar." She waved her hand. "Anyway, one clichéd hot night of passion resulted in...well, me."

"They didn't marry?"

She shook her head. "No. When my mom found out she was pregnant, she told my father. He covered all prenatal and birth expenses but she refused child support. He wasn't a part of the picture until I became a teenager and started getting into trouble. Then out of the blue Mom called my father and...well, he took over from there."

Sam's chewing slowed. He'd heard a lot of stories in his lifetime, but that had to be one of the stranger ones he'd borne witness to.

She nodded as she picked another carton up and transferred her chopsticks into it. "I know, weird, isn't it?"

"Are you close with them?"

"Them, as in my parents? Oh, I don't know. I'm close with my mom, I guess. My dad..." She grimaced. ''Well, let's just say that at fifteen it's hard to create a parental relationship from scratch.''

''That's majorly screwed up. What were you told about him until then?''

''That he was a successful doctor who lived in Beverly Hills.'' She shrugged. ''That's it.''

He stared at her.

She smiled. ''You'd have to know my mom to understand. Even though she accepted help during her pregnancy and my birth…well, she's a proud woman.''

''And your dad?''

''My dad was married to another woman when she contacted him.'' She made a face. ''Since then he's been married to three other women.''

''Yikes.''

She laughed at his choice of words. ''Yes, that about sums it up.'' She shifted so she was facing him. ''So tell me how your parents messed up your life.''

''They didn't. They still live in the same house I grew up in in Ohio. Married nearly forty years. I have one younger sister who moved to L.A. to live with me because she wanted to go to UCLA. And…well, that's about it.''

''That's it, huh?''

''Uh-huh. Pretty boring stuff, really.''

''And your becoming a doctor?''

''My sister's to blame for that. I needed a good

job. There were all those expenses involved in taking care of her, you know.''

''Your parents didn't help?''

''My parents couldn't help. My dad worked and still works in an automobile factory and my mom is a first-grade teacher.'' He gestured with his sticks after he filled his mouth with another potsticker. ''Anyway, I was just joking about the taking care of my sister part. I became a doctor because Heather was born with a severe cleft palate and the surgeon botched the job.''

''Heather being your sister.''

He nodded.

''She okay now?''

''Oh, yeah. More than okay. Now she's a regular pain in the ass. You know, like any other younger sister.''

Sam digested what he'd said along with the food. He'd never before shared with a date his sister's past and his motivation for becoming a plastic surgeon. And he wasn't all that sure why he had shared it now. What he did know was that it felt good to talk to someone outside his family about it. Correction. It felt good talking to Layla about it.

He noticed her smiling.

''What?''

She shook her head. ''Oh, I don't know. That's not what I expected from you, that's all.''

He twisted his lips. ''Let me guess. You thought

I'd become a plastic surgeon because of the poster I had of Farrah Fawcett up on my wall as a teen.''

She laughed then covered her mouth with her hand. ''Yes, that would be hitting pretty close to the mark.''

He put his food down, having had more than his fill. ''I became a plastic surgeon because of my sister. I became a nose, breast and butt man because that's where the money is.''

She gave him an exaggerated frown.

He merely grinned at her. ''Now, I think it's time for dessert.''

Layla looked around the coffee table. ''Do you mean fortune cookies? Because I didn't see anything sweet.''

Sam took the carton out of her hand, gave her a chance to swallow the bite in her mouth, then tackled her to the couch. ''Oh, I see lots of sweet stuff…''

Layla giggled. But that happy sound soon turned into a low moan as Sam nuzzled her neck then kissed her deeply. His fingers inched up under her shirt, seeking and finding her breasts. Just as he'd thought. She wasn't wearing a bra. He started to edge up the soft cotton so he could begin feasting on his dessert when she caught the hem, holding her shirt in place.

Sam cocked a brow at her, noticing the splashes of color high on her cheeks.

''Not with the lights on.''

''That doesn't make any sense. The lights were on at my place last night.''

''Mmm. And so was my camisole.''

He realized she was right. Until they'd traded rug burns for smooth sheets and the darkness of his bedroom, she had worn her camisole. He had yet to see her breasts in clear light.

''What's the matter? Do you have a third nipple?''

She smiled at him as she undid the button of his jeans. ''No. Nothing like that. It's just that considering who you are, and what you do, I'd prefer you not comparing my modest breasts to the bazoombas you create.''

Sam grinned. ''Bazoombas?''

She nodded. ''Uh-huh.''

She finished opening his jeans and slid her fingers inside his boxers. ''Now, where's that dessert you promised?''

All coherent thought scattered from Sam's mind as she stroked him to a hard, fevered pitch then pressed her hips upward against his so that the V of her jeans cradled him.

Oh, screw it. They could deal with the breast issue later....

6

THE BELL of Reilly's Sugar 'n' Spice Pastry Shop reminded Layla of a time she suspected really only existed in Jimmy Stewart movies. And this morning was no exception. She pushed open the door and gingerly stepped inside, the latest gossip rag tucked under her arm. It was seven-thirty and she didn't really have all that much time, but she craved something sweet and rich and fatally fattening. Of course that would have nothing to do with Sam's idea of dessert last night. That one had taken a good three hours to eat and left them both exhausted and dead to the world by two that morning.

She'd woken up a half hour ago to find him gone, a fortune cookie left on his pillow.

''You're wearing slacks.''

Layla blinked at Reilly, who'd stepped from the back of the shop carrying a fresh batch of sticky buns. There were few things better than a good friend and sticky buns. Put them together and you had the perfect combo for a damn good start to any morning.

She beamed at her friend and ordered a bun and five minutes of her time, pronto.

Reilly readied a tray that included coffee and carried it to a tall table with two bar stools near the front window. The morning sun was just beginning to stream through, making the spot warm and cozy.

Layla winced as the fabric of her slacks slid against her knees. It turned out that couch burns could be just as nasty as rug burns, especially when the rug burns were still raw. Not that she'd noticed at the time. It wasn't until she'd put a skirt on that morning and looked in the full-length mirror on the back of her closet door that she'd realized she wouldn't be able to wear a skirt for a while.

"Are you okay?" Reilly asked, eyeing her while adding sugar substitute to her coffee. Apparently she'd caught Layla's wince.

Layla tucked her loose hair behind her ear and smiled. "Fine." And she was fine. More than fine, actually. Certainly nowhere near letting a couple of rug and couch burns get in the way of her good mood. So she'd have to wear pants for the next few days. No big deal. Her smile widened. The reward had been more than worth it.

"Uh-oh. I know that look," Reilly said, slowly putting down her cup and leveling a stare at her friend.

And therein lay the difference between Reilly and Mallory. Where Mallory would be instantly satisfied that, well, Layla had been satisfied, Reilly was on "all men are dogs" alert.

''The last time you had that look you'd just gone out with Dr. Sleazeball for the first time.''

Layla made a face and picked apart her sticky bun, dividing it into bite-sized pieces. ''You would have to bring him up and spoil everything.''

Reilly shrugged as she sipped on her coffee, noticeably ignoring her own sticky bun. ''I just wish I'd said something then. You know, before you got yourself into so much trouble.''

''I wasn't in any trouble.''

''Not from a legal standpoint, no. Although nowadays you're lucky you didn't end up in court. I just read about a case the other day where the wife of a cheating husband was suing the mistress for willful and malicious assault on her happy marriage. Or something like that, anyway. She's asking for seven figures for pain and suffering.''

Layla grimaced. ''What a shocker.''

''But emotionally… God, Layla. Please tell me you're not going out with him again.''

Layla nearly choked on the pastry in her mouth. She used coffee to wash it down. ''God, no.''

Reilly's posture relaxed. ''You don't know how relieved I am to hear that. You know, that you're not going out with him again.'' She wrapped both hands around her cup.

''What would make you think that, anyway?''

Reilly shrugged. ''I just don't want you in that kind of situation again. It can get so messy, and all the sneaking around and lying…''

Layla considered her. "What's going on, Reilly?"

Reilly's hazel eyes looked tortured and relieved at the same time. "Two of my customers are involved in just that kind of mess."

"Don't tell me. The wife and the mistress."

Reilly propped her elbow on the table and shielded her eyes. "Bingo. For the past month or so, both of them have come in within ten minutes of each other every morning. Then this morning— *bam!*—they both ended up in here at the same time." She gave a visible shudder. "It was all I could do not to run out the front door screaming."

"What happened?"

Reilly dropped her hand and picked up her cup again. "Nothing. Neither knows the other exists."

"So why the big deal?"

"*I* knew." She frowned into her cup. "And they also seemed to hit it off. One commented on the other one's handbag, and within a blink they were chatting about shopping and clothes and…men. Without a clue that they were discussing the same man."

"I still don't see what the big deal is."

Reilly stared at her. "What if you'd crossed paths with Colton's wife without knowing it, struck up a conversation with her, then found out afterward she was Colton's wife?"

The bun didn't sit all that well in Layla's stomach. "Yikes."

"So now you get where I'm coming from."

Layla wiped her fingers on a napkin. "I think you should have introduced them."

Reilly's eyes nearly popped out of her head and plopped into her coffee cup. "Are you insane?"

"No, really." Layla shifted on her stool. "The wife would never have known who the mistress was, but the mistress would have probably figured out it was the wife. Well, if she had a half a brain in her head, anyway." She sighed. "If someone had done that for me, it would have saved everyone a whole lot of pain and heartbreak."

"No, it wouldn't have. It just would have made it public. Besides, if I recall correctly, the only one with the pain and heartbreak was you. Mr. Can't-Keep-His-Johnson-in-His-Pants moved on to an anesthesiologist the day after you called it quits."

Layla stiffened. "God, what are you? A walking personal history book?"

"Sorry. That's what happens when you don't have much of a personal life of your own and you get too acquainted with your customers' lives."

"And your friends'."

"And my friends'."

Layla finished off the rest of her bun in silence. Before meeting Sam the other night, Jim Colton hadn't crossed her mind in, oh, a good five or six months. *Liar.* Okay, so maybe he had. But only because it was hard to miss the nonstop gossip circulating about him at the Center. And because she was still so…horrified that she'd fallen into the married-guy trap.

"We're separated, have been for months." "My attorney's filing for divorce next week." "We both know it's been over for a long time now. We're only together because of the kids."

She cringed. Every tired old line in the book. And she'd fallen for every last one.

She felt…well, stupid.

At least she'd had her friends Reilly, Mallory and Jack to help pull her through the experience. She supposed that a lot of women who had gone through the same thing hadn't had someone to turn to. She, on the other hand, had plenty of someones. Mallory had suggested they pay a heavy to break Colton's kneecaps, actually using the word *heavy* as if stuck in a retro film festival. Reilly had been compassionate and understanding, cooing and stroking and feeding her. And Jack…

What had been Jack's reaction?

She tried to recall.

Silence.

That's it.

No, wait, he had said something along the lines of "I told you all men are pigs." Then he'd fallen silent.

Interestingly enough, he seemed to fall silent a lot when talk turned to the opposite sex.

"So if it isn't Colton, who is it?" Reilly asked.

Layla looked at her watch and shot to her feet,

her pants rasping against her abraded knees. She'd have to put some gauze on them when she got to work. "God, I'm late."

But not so late she couldn't stop and watch a size-two six-foot-tall blonde walk in the front door and eye the pastries in the display cases.

Layla looked at Reilly. *"B,"* she said, for bulimic.

"L," Reilly said, for laxative.

Either way, Layla figured the transgression would be worth it. Reilly made damn good sticky buns.

"I'll call you later," Layla promised.

Reilly gave her a brief hug. "You'd better."

"I will. If simply because we have to work on getting you a man so you don't spend so much time thinking about everybody else's."

HEATHER'S favorite lunch spot was the Santa Monica Pier and lunch included two hot dogs fully loaded and French fries laden with chili sauce. Dessert was an extra-large tangle of pink cotton candy.

Sam handed her the cotton candy, trying not to think of what form dessert had come in last night and failing.

Damn, but Layla was delectable in every sense.

Heather held out to him the pink cloud that looked a little too much like an old woman's hair, and he shook his head. "I'll pass," he said. "If I go into cardiac arrest and die I don't want the coroner to find that pink stuff in my stomach."

Heather smiled widely. "You're right."

He squinted at her in the bright sunlight.

She shrugged as they walked along the pier, gulls diving, sea lions squealing on a nearby buoy. "Well what I have to tell you may give you a heart attack. But, don't worry, I can deal with that. I do know CPR, you know."

"Yeah, I know. I paid for the course, remember?" He rubbed his churning stomach, wondering if it was just him, or if he couldn't handle spicy, greasy food the way he once had. "So go ahead. Now's as good a time as any to kill me."

She laughed, then turned around so that the wind was at her back, blowing her white-blond hair over her shoulders. "Who's the girl?"

"Girl?"

"Yeah, the one you cooked dinner for the other night."

"I didn't cook dinner for anyone, and she isn't a girl."

"You mean she was above the age of consent? Now that's a first."

He reached to take her cotton candy away from her. "Look who's talking."

"There's a difference between acting your age and actually being that age. And you," she poked her finger into his chest, "big brother, need to learn that."

The motion and the banter reminded Sam of similar scenes between him and his sister. A decade his junior, Heather had always been wiser than her years. And she'd always had a thing for sticking her finger into his chest. He remembered the first time she'd done it, he'd been thirteen and she'd been three and she'd had to get up on a chair in order to do it. It had been the cutest damn thing he'd seen up until that point. And it wasn't any less cute now.

She turned so that they were facing in the same direction again, linking her arm with his. "So who is she?"

"Who is who?"

She edged her arm into his side. "This woman you invite over to your place in the middle of the night."

Sam grimaced. He didn't share many of the women he dated with his family. In fact, his sister and parents had stopped asking years ago who he was seeing and when he planned to get married. As Heather once told him, they knew he'd tell them when it was time.

"I thought you were the focus of this lunch," he said, staring down at the top of her blond head.

She shrugged. "Maybe. But that doesn't mean I don't get to find out some things about you first."

"She's a doctor."

Heather raised her brows, too cute for her own good, despite the crooked scar that marred her upper lip. "If this involves stethoscopes and tongue depressors, I don't think I want to hear it."

He chuckled and pulled her tighter to his side, the

wind kicking the smell of the Pacific around them. ''I don't know what it involves yet. I've only seen her twice.''

''Where did you take her?''

He blinked. Now there was a question. And beyond ''bed'' he didn't have an answer.

''Nowhere,'' he decided on.

''You said you've seen her twice. That means dates, right? Which usually involves going out somewhere.''

He rubbed his chin with his other hand. ''We've seen the inside of my place…and hers.''

''No dinner?''

''I had pizza delivered the first night, but somehow we never got around to eating it. And last night was Chinese take out.''

Heather rolled her eyes. ''Big spender.'' She sighed melodramatically. ''You know, one of these days you're going to figure out that life is not simply about sex, Sam.''

''Pardon me?''

''You heard me. I mean, my God, have you ever had a relationship with a woman that didn't involve sex?''

He scratched his head. ''There's you.''

''I'm your sister. That doesn't count.''

He chuckled.

''I'm serious, Sam. Sex, sex, sex. That's all you think about. When's the last time you dated someone you didn't sleep with on the first date and every date thereafter?''

Sam opened his mouth, then snapped it shut again. There was... No, wait, the...

''Can't remember, can you?''

''Maybe that's because I don't judge relationships by how much sex they involve.''

She leveled a gaze at him. ''Well, maybe it's time you started.''

''What, playing by some kind of rule book like you women do? You know, no sex on the first date? Not going to happen.''

Heather shook her head. ''That's not what I mean at all. I'm just saying that if every now and again you tried to control yourself, looked beyond the sex and instant gratification that...well, maybe you'd find you actually liked the person.''

''And in order to do this I have to not have sex with her?'' He tried to imagine not having sex with Layla and felt his lungs freeze up.

Heather laughed. ''I'm not saying not have sex with them at all. I'm merely saying that you may want to concentrate as much attention on other aspects of the relationship. Let me ask you another question. Have you ever just kissed a girl goodnight without having sex with her?''

Sam thought a minute. ''Sure. When things are on the downslide and the thing is basically over.''

''Thing.'' She shook her head. ''God, you can't

even say the word *relationship,* can you? You're even worse than I feared.''

''What do you mean? I don't have a commitment problem. It's just that I haven't met the right person yet.''

''Yeah, well, how are you going to know if someone's the right person if all you're seeing are body parts?'' She elbowed him again. ''Maybe you wouldn't wake up all the time wondering what you were doing with a woman and feeling like you didn't know them at all if you actually tried having a civilized conversation with them.''

''Ouch.''

She smiled. ''I calls 'em as I sees 'em.''

''Mmm,'' he agreed. ''So are you going to share the reason for this luncheon meeting or are you going to keep it a secret and blackmail me into coming out here again?''

She laid her head against his shoulder and smiled up at him. ''I'm surprised you haven't figured it out for yourself. Then again, you never were the most observant person, were you?''

He stared at her.

She held up her left hand and wiggled her fingers. Her ring finger was no longer bare.

The hot dogs they'd eaten rushed back up his throat with a vengeance.

Heather took her arm from his and grinned down at the tiny band of gold with a diamond chip in the middle. She appeared happier than Jennifer Lopez sporting her latest twenty-carat engagement ring.

And Sam couldn't have been sadder.

"He asked me last weekend after dinner."

"The same dinner where he drank a twelve-pack of beer by himself?"

Heather's smile slipped, but only momentarily.

She slid her arm through his again and sighed. "It was the most romantic thing. I was up to my elbows in clay in the garage and he came in, sat on the bench behind me, and asked me to marry him."

The kind of proposal all little girls dream of, Sam thought, wondering if it was the beer breath, the three-day shadow or the ten-dollar ring that had won his sister over.

"So?" she said quietly. "Aren't you going to say anything?"

Sam realized he hadn't breathed a positive word since she'd shared the bad news and wondered if he could. Despite the way he felt, he would feel like a heel to be the one to wipe that smile from her face altogether.

Too late. It was already gone.

"You're upset," she said simply.

Upset didn't begin to cover it.

They'd stopped walking. Moments ago the wind had made them seem wrapped up in their own little familial cocoon, but now it amplified the tension building between them. "Don't you think you're rushing into this?"

Heather laughed. "We've been living together for two years, Sam. How much more time do you want us to take?"

"Long enough for you to see Brian for the worthless piece of crap he is."

In his entire life, nothing had ever affected Sam more than the shine of tears in Heather's eyes. Especially when he knew he was the one responsible for putting them there.

Damn.

"Look, I know you and Brian...don't get along."

"That's putting it mildly."

"But I at least thought you'd be happy for me."

Truth was, he hurt for her. More than she'd ever know.

She deserved so much better.

"You know, I think Mom's right. Nobody will be good enough for me in your eyes."

He blinked at her. "You've told Mom and Dad?"

She nodded, tucking her chin into her chest to keep him from seeing her tears. She turned and ran her sleeve across her eyes, the skirt of her denim dress wiping around her skinny legs. "Yeah. And seeing as Dad has all those health problems and won't be able to make the wedding..."

God, first an engagement, now a wedding day had been set? Sam was afraid he might end up having that heart attack after all.

She nailed him with those clear blue eyes. "I want you there, Sam."

He realized he'd been thinking of ways to get Brian out of her life for good. Paying him off. No, that wouldn't work. The jerk would drink his way through the money and end up back on Heather's doorstep. Setting him up with another woman. No, Heather would take his dirtbag butt back anyway. Hiring someone to mastermind an accident...

He caught the strange direction of his thoughts and turned toward the churning autumn waves of the Pacific.

"The wedding's a month from today," he heard his sister say quietly behind him. "I'd like you to give me away."

"To that moron? Not a chance."

He turned away and curved his fingers into fists, waiting for her to rail at him, curse him, say something, anything.

Instead, her parting words sounded so soft, so mournful, they hurt more than seeing her tears.

"You can't choose who you love, Sam." He felt her hand briefly on his back. "One day you're going to realize that. I only hope you figure it out before you lose the one you love."

Sam stood for a long time staring out at the ocean.

When he turned around Heather was nowhere to be seen.

He watched a dark-haired girl of about seven walk by with a boy of around ten. She was carrying a puff of cotton candy nearly as big as her as the boy casually reached out and stopped her from walking head-on into a low bench.

Sam squinted, trying to make his sister out in the distance. Unfortunately what was coming was one bench he wasn't going to be able to stop his sister from tripping over.

7

NINE O'CLOCK and all was definitely not well.

Layla closed the chart in front of her. She'd just examined six-year-old twins with chicken pox, and had sent them home with their mother along with detailed instructions and medication. She slid the chart into the slot for Lupe to pick up. Then she made her way to the back of the clinic where her buddy Jack—full name, Jack Daniels—was on his back on the floor trying to fix the bathroom sink.

She leaned against the doorjamb and crossed her arms. "Any luck?"

At thirty with light-brown hair and brown bedroom eyes, Jack was, by all rights, a man women salivated over. Except for her, Mallory and Reilly. Given the way they'd met three years ago, and the fact that all three of the friends of the female gender had been interested in the one male...well, they'd all agreed that friendship would be the best route.

Layla smiled, glad they'd come to that decision, because she could not only call the three of them friends, but her best friends.

And it sure came in handy that one of them could

wield a wrench with some skill, though Jack's real job was that of a columnist for *L.A. Monthly*.

"Almost done."

Layla thought it should be sacrilegious, somehow, to watch the impressive biceps of one of her best friends as he worked under the sink. But she was only human, after all. And as long as no one caught her, well, it was all good, wasn't it?

Lupe materialized next to her and elbowed her in the ribs. So much for no one catching her. She looked at the nurse, expecting a grin. Oh, she was wearing a grin all right. But it was a man-eating grin all for Jack.

"They don't make buns like that anymore," she said, clucked her tongue, then headed back down the hall.

"What's that?" Jack dropped the wrench and hauled himself out from under the sink.

Layla blinked. "What?"

"I thought I heard the word *buns*."

She gestured with her right hand. "Lupe was just saying that, um, she needed to stop at the market on the way home to pick up some hotdog buns."

Jack's grin told her he knew exactly what Lupe had said *and* where both women's attention had been focused.

Layla rolled her eyes. "God, you're such an egomaniac."

"Nope," he said, rising to his feet to test his handiwork. "I just like to see you blush."

"I don't blush."

His fix held, so he went ahead and began washing his hands, lathering up the side of his arms nearly to the sleeves of his faded blue T-shirt. "You do, too. In fact, you're blushing now."

Layla made a face and sat down on the closed commode. "Maybe I'm running a fever."

"Mmm. Maybe."

His deadpan expression told her he wasn't buying it.

"So," she said, changing the subject, "you never did fill me in on Mallory's car trouble. Will she be riding the Metro for the foreseeable future?"

He shook his handsome head as he dried himself off with a towel she handed him. "I swear, the three of you keep me around just to play Mr. Fix-It."

Layla pretended to be appalled by the suggestion. Then she cleared her throat. "So, will she?"

He chuckled then tossed the towel at her so it landed on her head. "No. I greased the gears in her tranny. But that's only a temporary fix. She's either going to have to get another car or have the transmission on that Yugo rebuilt."

Layla frowned as she folded the towel. "She can't afford either option, can she?"

Jack bent over to collect his tools, giving her another primo view of his buns. "If she gets the backing for that border documentary, she will."

Layla followed him out of the bathroom and

down the hall to her office. "May I?" he asked, gesturing toward the phone.

"Sure, sure. Go ahead. Just so long as you're not calling Bora-Bora."

"Ah, caught me."

She smiled.

He made his call.

Layla pretended to be busy doing other things, but was tuned in to the fact that he had to be calling a woman. His lowered voice gave it away.

He hung up.

"New girl?"

Jack grinned. "A gentleman doesn't kiss and tell."

"And who says you're a gentleman?" She leaned against her desk nodding toward Lupe as she passed by the door holding up three fingers for room three. "What border documentary?"

Jack stared at her. "You know. That one she's been working on for three months."

Layla tucked her hair behind her ear. Surely she hadn't been that out of it?

"Anything else I can do you for?" he asked, looking at his watch. "'Cause, you know, I do have someone waiting."

Lupe appeared in the doorway again.

"We're just finishing up," Layla told her. "One more minute."

"Actually, I think this is going to take longer than

a minute,'' Lupe told her. ''Because this isn't about any patients.''

Layla grimaced at her.

Then she nearly fell face-first to the white tile as Lupe stepped aside and revealed Sam Lovejoy behind her with a stuffed animal and a pizza box in his arms.

''Surprise,'' he said, a wholly devilish grin on his face.

Jack elbowed Layla. ''Appears I'm not the only one who has someone waiting…''

THE SURPRISE went both ways.

Sam glanced from the petite, round Hispanic woman who had led him to the office, then to Layla's stunning and stunned face, trying like hell to ignore that another man was standing next to her.

''Sam!'' Layla finally said, her voice barely above a whisper.

Silence fell among the group. Then the nurse looked at Layla and said, ''I was wrong. I guess they make them like that more often than I realized. A veritable smorgasbord of great buns, I tell you.''

He didn't get it. But he wasn't trying to get it, either.

''Jack Daniels,'' the other man said, extending his hand.

Sam moved the stuffed animal to sit on top of the pizza box and shook his hand. ''No, it's pizza,'' he said, an eyebrow raised.

"That's my name. Jack Daniels."

He looked over to see Layla still stunned. "Oh. Sam Lovejoy." He grinned. "And, yes, that's my name."

Sam eyed Jack for a long moment, but he didn't blink. Finally, Jack turned to Layla and kissed her on the cheek. "Let me know if you have any more problems with your, um, plumbing," he said.

Jack's gaze met Sam's over Layla's shoulder, a decidedly suggestive gleam there.

"Yeah, I will. Thanks," Layla said.

The room was silent after Jack left.

"Plumbing?"

"Huh?"

"He said to call if you had any more problems with your, um, plumbing."

She blinked, then seemed to focus on him and the situation. "Oh, yeah. He fixed the bathroom sink."

"Alone?"

"What are you doing here?" she asked, appearing not have heard his last question.

Sam shifted on his feet. He hadn't been all that sure she'd welcome a visit from him at the clinic, but as the night had worn on, and nothing short of a seven-point-something earthquake could have distracted him, he'd decided to drop by. He'd picked up the pizza and bought the stuffed animal bearing the pizza place's logo on the front as an afterthought.

Of course, he'd never expected to find another man already here.

The Mexican woman snuck up behind him. Sam felt something brush him from behind.

"Mmm. Definitely don't make them that way anymore," she said as she left again.

Layla got that shocked expression again then laughed.

Sam glanced behind him. "I think your nurse just goosed me."

"I think she just did, too."

He glanced around the place, finding the equipment outdated, the floor chipped and the walls in need of a good coat of paint. He put the pizza on top of a filing cabinet and held out the stuffed animal. "Dinner."

"Looks appetizing."

"The pizza, not the bear."

"I knew what you meant," she said as she picked up a pile of charts and looked through them, placing one that was on the bottom on the top.

Sam cleared his throat, suddenly feeling awkward and out of place. Which was a first for him. He usually felt comfortable wherever he was. "You know, I could probably get somebody to run some sort of fund-raiser for this place."

She stared at him.

"Looks like you could use some updating."

"We could use another doctor."

He put his hands in his pockets. "Just trying to help."

She smiled then slapped a chart into his stomach. Air exited his mouth in a whoosh as he scrambled to catch the chart. "I was hoping you would say that. Sore throat in room one."

Sam began to open his mouth, to tell her he hadn't done any general practice work in well over a decade, not since back when he'd interned. But she'd passed him, leaving nothing but the scent of vanilla and lemon in her wake as she disappeared through a door marked room three.

Maybe he was a good guy after all.

Layla watched Sam tousle the hair of a two-year-old in his mother's arms, the young patient the last for the night. Oh, she knew Sam was good in bed. And he made her smile. But given that his chosen path in life included sucking fat out of women's thighs…well, she'd had her doubts about his capacity for any real compassion.

As soon as the mother and child were out of sight, he closed the door to room two then collapsed against it, running his hands through his hair. He caught her watching him from the doorway of her office and offered up a grin. "Now that's what I call a date."

She laughed, moving out of the way as Lupe retrieved her coat from the office and told them both good-night.

"Is that what you came here for? A date?" she asked, crossing her arms over her chest.

"I came here to feed you and ask you out on a date."

She glanced at her watch. It was almost eleven-thirty. "My place in ten?"

"No, next Friday night at seven."

She hiked a brow. "You weren't expecting to see me until next Friday?"

"No, I wanted to ask you out on an official date for next Friday because my sister thinks I need to take you out." He grinned. "Of course I want us to get together before that though. The pizza and bear prove I can't go a day without wanting to see you."

He still stood a mile away from her, but his words made her feel as if he was a breath away.

"Black tie?"

"Yeah. I figured the forewarning would give you enough time to find the right dress. You know, preferably something slinky with lots of slits."

"Ah," she said, wondering if she should be insulted, then deciding not to be.

Black-tie events and the whole Hollywood scene was so not her thing. She rubbed her arms through her jacket. But she couldn't bring herself to refuse him outright considering he had just spent the past two-and-a-half hours helping out at the clinic.

Besides, she was curious to get a look at his life beyond the bedroom door. A large schism existed between what she'd thought she'd known about him before and what she was coming to know about him now.

"On one condition," she said quietly.

He hiked up both brows and pushed from the door. "Tonight didn't earn me enough points?"

She grinned. "When I say 'now' we leave."

He came to stand directly in front of her, causing her pulse to leap in response to his nearness. "Hmm. I have a condition of my own."

Layla swallowed hard.

"We stay at least a half hour before 'now' enters the equation."

"Deal."

Naughty intent flickered over his face, chasing exhaustion from her muscles and replacing it with hot desire.

What had she used to do before he'd entered her life? she wondered, allowing her gaze to slide over his handsome features, down his forever-quirked brows, his straight nose, his full, kissable mouth. As they stood there, close enough to touch but not touching, she idly compared her life to photographs. There were the black-and-white shots of her running from job to job, living in a vacuum of sorts. A rewarding vacuum but a vacuum just the same.

Then there was life with Sam. A vivid color print with flames licking around the edges.

Although she essentially hadn't slept more than a couple of hours in three straight days, she wanted to jump his bones right here and now and go at it until she couldn't go anymore.

He leaned forward, his mouth brushing against hers lightly. Then again, increasing her heart rate and making her feel hot all over. She understood all too well that Sam had only been in her life for a few short days. And that tomorrow that snapshot of her life could slip back to black-and-white. But she consciously made the decision to romp around for a while in the colorful palette he provided her with without thought of yesterday or tomorrow, only the sweet few moments of now.

He was a great kisser. His tongue flicked out, licking the corners of her mouth, then delving between her lips, smoothly invading the depths then retreating so he could start all over again.

Definitely a great kisser.

Layla sighed and began to melt against him. He caught her shoulders in his hands, holding her back.

"Good night, Dr. Hollister."

Layla blinked at him. Good night? Just like that? She'd been convinced they'd go back to her place. Nuke the leftover pizza in the box in her office. Change the sheets together then have all kinds of fun getting them dirty again...

She watched as Sam shrugged out of the borrowed lab coat, hung it in her office, then walked from the clinic with a grin and a wave.

"Huh?" she said, deciding to stand right where she was and think about that one for a minute.

8

"So LET ME get this straight," Mallory said, sitting cross-legged in the middle of Layla's living-room floor two days later, looking like a Kewpie doll drafted into combat with her curly dark hair and camouflage pants and short black boots. Definitely not your run-of-the-mill Hollywood look. "Dr. Lovejoy asked you out to some posh black-tie event a week from yesterday. Then he left you at the clinic after kissing you good night. Therefore, you turned down an invite to dinner for tonight."

Layla made a face, not liking where this was heading. This was the first time in over two weeks that she and her three friends had all gotten together and she wanted to…she didn't know. To laugh, maybe? Watch an old movie? Play Scrabble? Something, anything but discuss the odd state of her love life.

Yet here they were. Mallory on the floor with her military apparel and a black T-shirt emblazoned with the words Being a Woman Isn't Easy: It Requires Dealing With Men. Reilly sitting on the couch next to her wearing a flowing flowery dress, her legs tucked underneath her. And Jack looking out of place yet very right in snug jeans and a T-shirt, sitting in the old wood rocking chair off to the side, pretending not to be listening to them while flicking through the muted channels on TV, as he usually did when the topic turned to men.

"I turned him down because I was getting together with you guys tonight," Layla said.

"Hmmph." Mallory loaded a corn chip with chunky salsa then crunched down on it.

"Do you know how many calories that one bite has?" Reilly asked, sipping on her diet soda.

"I don't know…a lot?" Mallory asked then swallowed.

Jack cracked a grin as he settled on ESPN.

Reilly leaned closer to the coffee table laden with munchies. "So Jack tells me this guy is pretty hot."

Layla looked at Jack who was gaping at Reilly. "I did not. I said he might be the type that some women find attractive."

Mallory waved him away, "Which is man-speak for get out the oven mitts. Anyway, is he really that plastic surgeon guy? The one reported to have fondled more breasts in Hollywood than all the male stars combined?"

Layla crossed her arms. "If I recall correctly, you're the one who reported that information."

"Doesn't make it any less true."

Reilly piped up, "She has a point."

Layla made a sound of exasperation. "What point? Somebody please tell me, because if there's a point hidden in there somewhere I didn't hear one.''

Her three friends looked at each other, then back at her.

''What?''

''Oh boy,'' Jack said, sitting back and folding his hands on his stomach.

''What is that supposed to mean?''

''That you're in deep,'' Reilly said.

''Up to your eyeballs,'' Mallory agreed.

Reilly put her feet on the floor and sat up. ''You never get angry with us, Lay. That means that what's going on between you and the boob doc…well, it's pretty serious.''

''Don't call him that,'' Layla muttered, flopping back onto the couch and squeezing her arms more tightly around her torso.

Long moments ticked by with everybody looking at everything but each other.

Then there was a sound suspiciously like a giggle from Reilly's direction.

Mallory joined in.

Then all three women were laughing.

Jack just stared at them, puzzled. ''I need another soda,'' he said, getting up and going to the door that led outside, which meant he was going for a cigarette. His one allowable addiction, he'd told them, even though they all pretended he had quit a few months back.

Mallory stopped laughing first and started shaking

her head. "I can't believe it. Fate is definitely not without a sense of humor." She pointed a finger at Layla. "You, of all people, falling for a tit-thigh-and-butt man."

"I didn't fall for him."

Reilly hiccupped. "Then what would you call it?"

"I don't know…" Layla twisted her lips. "Great sex?"

Mallory picked up her monster-size margarita, took a hefty sip, then licked the salt from her lips. "I, for one, say it's long past time." She shrugged. "So he's going about things a little backwards. So what?"

"Backwards?" Reilly asked.

"Well, yeah." She glanced at Layla. "Essentially, your first date was on the couch at his place, right?"

Jack had begun to walk back into the apartment, but mumbled about forgetting something, did an about-face and disappeared back outside again.

"Right," Layla said.

"Second date was here."

Reilly stared at her. "Please tell me you didn't do it on the couch."

Layla smiled at her.

"Eeeuw." She pushed from the couch and joined Mallory on the floor, apparently deciding that Mallory was right and grabbing a corn chip…sans sauce.

"So, in essence, the two of you skipped to step ten—wicked, uncontrollable sex—in the dating game, and he's just doing a bit of backtracking, that's all."

"You mean, he wants to date now?"

Jack finally braved the apartment and crossed to sit back in the rocking chair. "I don't get it. He's already got access to the good stuff. So why go back and do the boring stuff?"

All three women stared at him.

He held up his hands. "What? What did I say?"

"Actually, Jack has a point," Reilly said, brushing the salt from her hands. "Why would he want to backtrack? Why not just keep up the midnight rendezvous?"

Mallory sighed as if dealing with a particularly slow child. "Because where do you go from there?"

Reilly shrugged. "I don't know. Move in together?"

Layla nearly choked. "We just met."

"My point exactly!" Mallory exclaimed.

Layla rolled her eyes. "Mall, you keep making these points that none of us are getting."

Mallory shrugged as if their cluelessness was of no consequence to her and attacked the nachos next to the bowl of plain corn chips. "Just that there really is no reasonable place to go forward from here, so you have to go backward."

Layla tilted her head. "You know, he mentioned

that his sister thought it would be a good idea if he took me out.''

''He talked about you to his sister?'' Jack asked.

''Wow. This is serious,'' Mallory said gravely.

''Oh, come on.'' Layla got up from the couch and snatched the remote from Jack. She changed the channel to Lifetime. ''He's probably out with someone else as we speak.''

Someone with perfect bozoombas that even he himself may have had a hand in creating.

There was a knock at the door.

The four friends fell silent.

Layla rolled her eyes again. ''It's probably the neighbor come to complain about too much noise.''

''What noise?'' Mallory asked. ''We're not making any noise.''

Layla gave her friend a dirty look then bumped into the hall table, sending all her unopened bank and loan statements shuffling to the floor. She gathered them together then swung the door open to find Sam standing there grinning.

''Hi,'' he said, making her toes curl against the wood floor and nearly making her drop the statements she clutched to her chest.

''Told you it was serious,'' she heard Mallory say behind her.

''YOU KNOW, you just made my life completely impossible to live.''

Sam watched Layla's mouth as she spoke, but really didn't hear her words. All he knew was that the instant she'd opened the door, his own life made perfect sense again.

Which made absolutely no sense.

He stuffed his hands into his jeans pockets. "I was in the neighborhood and thought I'd drop in to say hi."

Lame, but, hey, a desperate guy couldn't be choosy.

"Come in," a woman with short curly dark hair said, waving at him from where she sat on the floor.

"Yes, do," the cute blonde next to her said.

"Why the hell not. You're all they're talking about anyway," mumbled the guy he'd met at the clinic a couple of nights ago.

Sam quirked a brow at Layla. Her cheeks were pink, her mouth utterly kissable and her body language telling him she'd like nothing more than to whack him.

Whoa.

She quietly cleared her throat as she carefully stacked a mass of envelopes she held to her chest on a hall table. "Just remember," she muttered, "you asked for this."

He squinted at her, unsure what she meant as she grasped his arm and tugged him inside.

Sam was glad the other guy had the rocker and that there was an open spot on the couch.

He sat down and stared at everyone staring at him.

"I'll go get you a soda," Layla said, crisscrossing the room. "Unless you want a margarita?"

Sam shook his head. "No, a soda ought to do it."

She disappeared. He tried to shake the feeling that she'd purposely orchestrated her exit.

Sam shifted until he leaned forward with his arms on his knees, his hands clasped between them. This was new territory for him. What kind of fool thing made him up and show up at her apartment after she had told him she couldn't see him that night? And surely after he saw she was having a night in with her friends, he should have politely excused himself, rather than accepting the invitation to join them. An invitation made mostly by her friends and hesitantly by Layla.

He'd had plenty to fill his day with. From doing 18 holes with his old mentor, to playing a game of doubles on one of the club's seventeen courts, to going out to dinner at one of L.A.'s posh restaurants. But all he could think about was what Layla was doing that minute and how soon time would pass so he could see her again...until he'd ended up at her door. And now here he sat returning the curious stares of three strangers.

Well, except for Jack over there, who was frowning into his root beer.

"Did you really do Demi Moore's breasts?" the cute blonde asked.

Sam grinned. "Pure rumor. I have it on good authority that they're real."

"Yeah, right," the brunette said, getting to her knees and extending her hand across the junk-food-laden coffee table. "Mallory Woodruff."

"Sam Lovejoy. But then, I guess you already know that." He considered her. "Do I know you?"

"Bad pickup line," the guy to his left said.

"That's only if it was meant as a pickup line," Sam corrected.

"Nearly two years ago. Documentary producer," Mallory said.

"Ah." Sam took his hand back. "The one who made me look like Mengele to the women's lib movement."

"Hi," the breathless blonde cut in. "I'm Reilly."

"Hi, Reilly," he said, deciding he liked her better than the prickly brunette who had given him snide nicknames in her piece. People still called him Silicone Man and Chop Doc.

"We've already met," Jack said.

"That, we have." Sam sat back on the couch, looking for Layla to return. "Any interesting plumbing stories to share?"

"Plumbing?" Reilly echoed.

Mallory may have looked innocent enough crunching on a corn chip, but her almost-yellow eyes were on him.

"Jack fixed Layla's sink at the clinic a couple of days ago," he explained.

"Ah," Mallory said simply.

"I'm a columnist for *L.A. Monthly*," Jack said.

The two other women stared at him as if surprised he'd offered up the information.

Male posturing. Women would never catch on.

"Ah, yes. Now the name rings a bell. I've read your stuff," Sam said. "Good, um, stuff."

"I've seen some of your work too," Jack said. "Good, um, stuff."

Reilly made a sound behind her hand while Mallory rolled her eyes to stare at the ceiling. "Men. Insufferable. You wouldn't know a real breast if it jumped up off a woman's chest and bit you."

"You're wrong there." Sam grinned at her. "You just make the mistake of thinking we give a damn."

He was somewhat surprised she didn't fling her margarita his way. Instead she smiled. "A man who can give as well as he gets." She looked at Reilly. "I give him a tentative thumbs-up."

"Thumbs-up?" Sam asked.

"Here you go," Layla said a little loudly as she came back into the room carrying two sodas. She handed Sam one and sat down next to him as she popped open the other. "So…you've all introduced yourselves?"

Sam suppressed a chuckle. Like she hadn't heard everything from two feet away in the kitchen.

"Did you all go to school together?" he asked.

Four blank looks.

He gestured over them with his soda before taking a slug. "Have you been friends for a long time?"

"Eons," Mallory said.

"Long enough," Jack offered.

"Three years," Reilly was more helpful.

He looked at Layla. "Three years," she agreed.

"It was the funniest thing, really," Reilly said, rising to her knees and sifting through the corn chips. "You've been to the clinic, right? Well, anyway, down the block is a police precinct where they do some of the disaster response training. Three years ago, Mallory was there filming a session. Jack was there writing it up. I had signed up as a victim and Layla had just started at the clinic and didn't know they did that kind of thing."

"Victim?" Sam asked.

Reilly nodded, looking remarkably like a glammed-down Jennifer Aniston with her pouty mouth and attractive features. "Part of the training exercise. They ask for volunteers to act out different scenarios. You know, earthquake victims and the like. They give us roles and we're supposed to act them out for the trainees."

"Shouldn't be hard to find volunteers in L.A., what with all the wanna-be actors," Sam said.

"Actually, it is difficult to get people involved. It doesn't pay," Reilly said. "That's why my sister ropes me into volunteering every year." She waved her slender hands. "Anyway, that particular year I was playing an asthmatic car accident victim with a crushed pelvis. They wedged me inside a wrecked car and everything. So there I am, trying to call for help when Layla comes rushing out of the clinic thinking I'm the real thing. I, of course, have no idea who she is. And Mallory and Jack are filming and watching. And it isn't until Layla gets the firefighters to put me on the street that she figures out the stuff on my head isn't real blood but a squib.''

Mallory sighed. ''It was a blood-filled condom with a hole poked in it, Reilly. A squib is when they use a small charge to emulate a gunshot in movies.''

Sam glanced up to find Layla smiling. ''Not my most shining moment,'' she admitted.

''Anyway, while all this is happening, a real car accident happens and Jack ends up pinned against a light pole. All of us went out to dinner that night and have been friends ever since.''

Sam looked at Jack who shrugged. ''Broken leg.''

''Bruised femur,'' Layla corrected.

''It's my leg. I'll relay the injury.''

Layla waved him away. ''If your leg had been broken, Jack, you wouldn't have been out having dinner with three crazy women the same night.''

He grinned. ''That's what you think. Visions of a foursome can be very inspiring.''

All three women rolled their eyes then laughed.

And for a flash Sam envied them.

It wasn't a word he was very familiar with, envy. But in that one moment, watching them correct and contradict each other and laugh together, he envied them their closeness, their friendship, their history. And he especially envied that Layla's three friends would probably know her better than he ever would.

"So how did the two of you meet?" Mallory asked.

Sam was jarred out of his thoughts by the question.

"He tried to pick me up in a bar," Layla said.

He balked. "Oh, fess up, Layla. It was you who tried to pick me up in that bar."

"Bar?" Reilly asked.

Sam went on to relay the fateful night he'd met Layla in a way that made the pink in her cheeks darken to red, and made him want to disappear into her bedroom and pull her with him.

Mallory waggled her finger at Layla. "You little hussy you. I knew there was a side to you that you didn't let us see."

"As if the couch wasn't proof enough," Reilly said.

Everyone stared at her.

Jack pushed up from the chair. "Join me for a cigarette, Sam?"

"I don't smoke."

He gestured for him to come anyway. "Trust me, if you stay here for the next few minutes, you'll wish you did."

Sam got the impression that girl talk wasn't the only reason Jack wanted him to join him outside. He smiled at the three women watching him expectantly. "If you'll excuse me, ladies…"

Jack pulled the apartment door closed behind him then led the way downstairs and out into the courtyard. Sam watched him take a cigarette out of his front pocket, smooth the length with his fingers then tuck the end into his mouth.

Sam squinted into the diffused rays of the setting sun. "Why am I getting the impression that you're going to ask me what my intentions are?"

Jack chuckled as he blew out a long line of smoke. "Maybe because I am." He seemed to consider Sam long and hard. "You know, Mall is not the only one who did a piece on you."

Sam nodded. "I know. I have your column, dated approximately two years ago, interestingly around the same time as the documentary, framed and hanging on my waiting-room wall." He took a deep breath. "Let's see if I can remember correctly. And I quote, 'Rather than being burned at the stake as some quasi-pro-women's groups would like to see done to Dr. Lovejoy, the guy ought to be given a medal.'" He rubbed his chin, warming to his subject. "I'm not sure of the wording of the rest, but you state that one reason you're a big supporter of my work is the confidence it gives to the women I've worked on."

Jack chuckled and nodded. "That about covers it." He took another drag off the cigarette, stared at the burning end, then pinched it off and put the rest of the unsmoked cigarette in his front shirt pocket. "What's interesting is that when I wrote the piece I never imagined you and me standing where we are right now."

"Meaning outside Layla's apartment."

"Yep."

"Let me guess. You wrote the piece to get back at Mallory."

"I wrote the piece to balance the playing field," Jack corrected. "But now that you're dating a really good friend of mine...well, I'm seeing you in a different light."

"And it's not very flattering."

"What would you say if I told you your sister was dating a plastic surgeon?"

"I'd say hallelujah. But that's a whole different story." He cleared his throat as he watched a young woman approach through the courtyard then let herself inside the door behind them. "But I know what you mean." He looked at the other man, feeling somewhat...glad, actually, that Jack thought enough of Layla to want to look after her. "Would it help if I told you that my intentions toward her are honorable?"

"Does the word *honorable* include couches?"

Sam barked with laughter. "You guys really do share everything, don't you?"

Jack grinned. "You have no idea."

"Okay, maybe *honorable* is not the word. Let's just say that I have no intention of hurting Layla."

Jack looked at him for a long moment, then finally he nodded. "I guess that will have to do, won't it?"

"And if it wouldn't have done?"

Jack opened up the door for him. "Well, then, I just would have had to open up a can of whoop ass on you and then you would have had to shop around for your own personal plastic surgeon."

Sam's amused response echoed through the stairwell of the apartment building.

"Go FISH," Reilly said three hours later.

Everyone at the table looked up from where they were playing five-card draw poker.

"It was a joke," she said. "Sure, you guys are all fun and games when there isn't any money on the table, but put a quarter up and you turn into a bunch of humorless Donald Trumps."

Layla glanced at where Sam dealt Reilly three more cards, watching his hands as he did so. He had incredible hands. Not because of what they looked like, but because of what they could do to her.

Three hours had passed since she'd found him grinning in her doorway. And somehow during that time he'd not only disarmed each of her friends one by one, he'd melded with the group as if he was one of them.

Of course, there were some important differences that came with his presence. One was that they were playing poker. Friends Night In had never included poker before. But when Sam had suggested it, and for some male-motivated reason Layla couldn't grasp, Jack had agreed, she, Mallory and Reilly had suffered through a half hour of instructions. She stared at the five, six, ten, jack and ace she held thinking Sam could spend the next week teaching her and she still wouldn't get it.

But the biggest difference was that she was so aware of his presence her very skin vibrated with his nearness.

"How many?"

Layla blinked at Sam, realizing she'd been staring and that he'd assumed she'd been paying attention. "Oh," she said, keeping the ace then picking three cards at random to throw down. "Three."

He dealt her cards then took care of Jack and picked up his own cards.

"A quarter," Mallory said, chucking one into the pot in the middle of the table.

Reilly followed suit. Sam put in a quarter then raised another one.

"So that means fifty cents for me, right?" Layla asked.

"Right," Sam said, sharing a long-suffering glance with Jack.

She looked at her cards. Two jacks. She added her money, only to have Jack up the ante even further.

Reilly threw her cards down. "Okay, it's past midnight and I'm no longer capable of pretending I know what's going on."

"Oh, come on, Rei," Mallory said, picking up her friend's cards. "If I can hang in there, so can you."

She frowned at Reilly's hand then put them back down.

"Actually, she's right. And I'm folding, too." She added her cards to the pile.

Sam and Jack looked at Layla.

"What? Oh." She added another quarter.

And, interestingly enough, her pair of jacks took the pot.

"Yes!" she said, sliding the pile of coins in her direction. "And I'm with the girls. I think it's time we called it a night."

Sam gave her that crooked smile. "What, you're not even going to give a guy a chance to win back his money?"

"Nope."

Jack chuckled and gathered up the cards.

A little while later, after Mallory and Jack, then Reilly had stumbled through the front door, and Layla had cleaned up the place with Sam's help, they stood in the middle of the living room staring at each other.

"So..." she said, feeling as if the temperature had shot up a hundred degrees within the blink of an eye.

He slid his hands into his pockets. "I had a good time tonight, Lay. Your friends are great. A little strange, but great."

She laughed. "Well, you know the saying. It takes one to know one."

"Yeah," he said.

"So," she repeated, about to gesture to the sofa and suggest they retire there and watch the DVD of *My Big Fat Greek Wedding* she'd rented for the night.

"So, I guess this is good night."

Sam leaned forward and kissed her, but Layla was so surprised by his words that she didn't get a chance to kiss him back as he withdrew and walked out the door.

"Huh?" she said, her fingers going to her lips as she stared at the empty air. All that, and he just kissed her and left? Seeing as this was the second time it had happened in three days...well, she was a hairbreadth away from getting a complex.

What was she talking about? She was well beyond complex phase. Right now she was wondering if she had a smear of something really awful across her face, or if Sam had decided that sex with her wasn't as enticing as he'd first thought it was.

Or it could be as Mallory had said. That Sam was backtracking in the dating game.

This wasn't making any kind of sense at all. None whatsoever.

She picked up the phone and dialed Sam's home number, knowing damn well he wouldn't be home, but not caring. She needed some answers and she wasn't going to stop until she got them.

9

WELL. This sucked dead canaries.

Sam turned off the shower, sighed, then turned the spray back on again, this time laying off the hot and going with full-blast cold.

He'd gotten home from Layla's and headed straight for the bathroom where he was putting himself through the most brutal anti-sex treatment known to man.

And to think **right** now he could be sinking into her slick flesh.

He leaned his closed fists against the shower wall and gritted his teeth, forcing himself to stay under the punishing spray until he couldn't stand it any longer. Then he finally switched the water off. He stood for long moments trying to catch his breath, then snatched a towel from a shelf and briskly dried off, heading into the living room after he'd tied the towel around his waist.

Sex, sex, sex. For a guy who'd never really given it much serious consideration before, it seemed it was all he thought about now that he was denying himself the pleasure.

Heather and her damn ideas.

He remembered Layla's sexily startled look when he'd kissed her good-night—again—without making a single pass, and he groaned. He grabbed the television remote and pressed the button to lower the theater screen, surfing through channels before it clicked into place. How was it that there were over a hundred-and-fifty channels on his satellite and he couldn't find one single thing he liked? He paused on a show focusing on quick decorating makeovers, cursed, then pressed the preset for ESPN.

Food. Maybe food would fill the craving.

He padded toward the kitchen, only then catching the blinking light on his new answering machine. He pressed the button and braced himself for his sister's voice.

Instead he got Layla's.

"Okay, Sam, you're going to tell me what's going on right now or...or..."

He could virtually see her searching her mind for something to say and grinned.

"Or I grab the next available guy and release all this sexual tension."

Not good.

He tapped the receiver and it flipped up so he could catch it in his hand—an old trick he'd learned in college. In two seconds flat the line to Layla's was ringing.

"Hello?"

"Are you alone?" he asked.

He could almost see her smile. "Yes. But you

caught me in the nick of time. I was just about to go out trolling.''

''Trolling, huh?''

''Mmm. It's an L.A. thing. You wouldn't know about it.''

''Wouldn't I?''

''Is this a booty call?''

Images of Layla's pert little bottom slid through his mind, completely undoing any good the showers had done. ''No.''

''Shame.''

Wasn't it, though?

There was a long silence during which he listened to her tapping something on her end of the line, then she finally said, ''Look, are you going to tell me what's going on, or are you going to leave me guessing?''

''Going on?''

''Answer my question with a question one more time and I'm hanging up.''

Tempting. It would mean he wouldn't have to deal with her question.

On the other hand, it might mean he wouldn't have to deal with her or her questions ever again.

''Fair enough.''

''So give.''

''I don't know what you're talking about.''

She made a sound of frustration that just about summed up how he was feeling.

"You didn't say anything about not playing dumb," he pointed out.

"So there is something going on, then. You'll admit that much."

"I'll admit to nothing."

"Come on, Sam. I'm not getting this. The first two nights we see each other, you couldn't keep your hands off me—"

"We couldn't keep our hands off each other."

"Right. The only difference being that the past couple of nights you haven't given me a chance to touch you. You've been too busy diving for the door."

He didn't say anything. Right now he was too occupied with watching the front of his towel tent out at the mere sound of her voice.

"And now...well, now you give me a peck on the lips, say good night and then disappear. Is it something I did? No, scratch that. That sounds desperate. I may be desperate but I'm not about to look it. Has something changed?"

"Changed? Oh, no, wait! Don't hang up." He cleared his throat and strode toward the kitchen where he took a bottle of cold water out of the refrigerator. "No, nothing's changed. Not really. I still want you as much as I did then. More, even."

"Then, why..."

He chugged the cold liquid until he had to stop and pull in a breath.

"Mallory says it's a backtracking of sorts."

"Mallory would know, of course."

She laughed faintly. "She said that seeing as things were going too far too fast for us, that we had no choice but to backtrack to earlier steps."

"Steps? Explain steps."

"You know, each phase in the dating game."

"Why am I getting a picture of Jim Lange, three chairs and a wood screen?"

"So that's not it."

"Not hardly."

"Then tell me what it is, because I'm really starting to get a complex over here, Sam."

He sighed and strode out to the couch where he'd first claimed her sweet little body. He flopped down on the leather and moved the receiver to his other ear. "Can't do that, Lay." He listened to her sound of frustration. "But there is something else I can do for you."

"If you're not here, I don't see how that's possible."

"Ah, ye of little faith. Where are you?"

"What do you mean, where am I? I'm at home."

He didn't respond.

"Oh, you mean inside my apartment? I'm in the living room."

"Good. Switch everything off and go into the bedroom."

He heard her moving around and realized she was doing as he asked. Which made his towel inch ever higher.

"Okay, I am now standing in my bedroom."

"Good. Now light a few of those candles you have around the place."

He heard a match strike then moments later she blew out the match. "Done."

Give him a few more minutes and he would be, too.

God, what had he been thinking when he'd decided to take Heather up on her challenge? Why in the world had he made the pact with himself not to have sex with Layla again until he got to know her a little better? Guilt. It was guilt, pure and simple. He felt guilty because of what he'd said to Heather about marrying Brian. He felt guilty that he hadn't talked to her since.

Guilt stunk.

But it was more than that, really, wasn't it? For some reason he had yet to define, his younger sister had always made him want to be a better person. Do better. Be better. She was why he'd become a cosmetic and reconstructive surgeon. She was the reason he wanted to put his reputation for womanizing behind him. She was the reason he hadn't thought twice about taking the position when he'd been invited on board at Trident Medical Center. Oh, he had been good at what he had done. Damn good. But she made him aim higher.

He only wished Heather could aim a little higher herself.

"Sam?"

The soft, sexy way Layla said his name made him groan. ''What?''

''Is that it, or do you want me to do, um, something else?''

Oh, he definitely wanted her to do something else. But what he had in mind required her to be in the same room, not across town.

He cleared his throat. ''Mmm. Okay. Now I want you to take off those sandals you're wearing.''

''I'm not wearing them anymore.''

''Good.'' He made a face. God, he sucked at this. The thought of the word *suck* made him want to groan. ''Have you changed out of your clothes yet?''

''No.''

''Okay, then, I want you to undo the buttons of your shirt.'' He imagined the little pearl buttons down the front of her white, sleeveless blouse. ''Slowly. One by one.''

''Sam...''

''Trust me,'' he murmured.

''Okay,'' she said after a long minute.

''No, don't take it off yet.''

He heard a sound and guessed she had taken her blouse off and was now putting it back on.

''Now,'' he said, sinking down farther into the cushions. ''I want you to undo that little clasp at the front of your bra.''

''With my shirt still on?''

''Shh. You're not allowed to say anything.''

"I'm not?"

"Shh."

"Okay."

He smiled against the receiver. He liked this. He liked this a lot.

"Mmm. Okay. This is what I want you to do now…"

He switched off his television then proceeded to give her whispered instructions. "Did you unclasp the front of your bra?"

"I thought I wasn't supposed to say anything?"

He cracked a grin. "A simple yes or no will be the extent of your vocabulary tonight. Do you think you can handle that, Dr. Hollister?"

"Yes."

"Good. Very good," he murmured, resting his feet on top of the magazines on his marble coffee table. "Now, I'll ask you again. Have you opened your bra?"

He heard a snap. "Yes."

Oh, God, just imagining her on the other side of the line with her blouse and bra open made his throat tighten.

"Okay, now, flatten your right hand on your stomach."

On that nice, flat, silk-covered stomach…

"I'm holding the ph—never mind. Okay."

He heard her switch the receiver from her right to her left hand.

"Are you doing as I asked?"

"Yes."

"Good. Very good."

Too good. He was supposed to be turning her on, but instead he was turning himself on.

"Mmm. Okay, now splay your fingers. That's it—stretch them until you can't stretch them anymore. Now, slowly...very slowly...inch them upward. That's right. In between your breasts and up toward your neck." He swallowed hard. "Now, bring them back down, moving toward the right. Down over the peak of your right breast. Over your straining nipple—"

She gasped and he grinned.

"Now, we can't allow for any jealousy, Lay, so what I want you to do is sweep your fingers ever so lightly over your left breast."

He didn't need to ask if she was doing what he told her. He knew she was.

"Now, with the very tip of your index finger, touch the edge of your areola. That's it. Now draw it around the circumference. Slowly, slowly. No, slower yet. Now again, drawing tighter circles until the pad of your finger is resting against the very tip..."

Oh, boy...

"Now put that same fingertip into your mouth. Rolling your tongue around and around, getting it nice and hot and wet."

He listened to her sucking sounds and said a silent prayer that he'd be able to finish what he'd started.

"That's it. Now draw that fingertip down over your jaw…your neck…your collarbone," she had a great collarbone, "and let it slide over your nipple."

He heard her take a shuddering breath and he did the same on his end.

There was a loud clank. He had to draw the receiver away from his head it was so loud.

Some rustling sounds then, "Sorry. I dropped the phone."

He grinned. "That's all right. Just let me know when you're back in position."

A moment later he heard her tentative, "Okay."

He had the perfect image of her standing alone in her candlelit bedroom, golden light flickering over her stomach and breasts, an expectant, enraptured expression on her beautiful face.

"Now, I want you to dip that finger down, Layla," he whispered. "That's right. Back over your stomach toward the snap of your shorts. No, no. Don't undo them. Instead, I want you to tuck your fingertip just inside the waistline." He paused for a heartbeat. "Now, budge your finger toward your side. Slowly. Ever so slowly…"

He heard her quick intake of breath and knew his directions were having the desired effect.

He cleared his throat. "Okay, now I want you to take your finger out and splay your hand over the front of your shorts, just below your waistband."

"Okay," she rasped, breaking the rule of silence

and letting him know that she was getting as restless as he was.

"Apply a little pressure and…stay like that until I tell you to move again."

Sam lulled his head back against the sofa, closed his eyes, then opened them again to stare at the ceiling.

"What are you doing right now?" she whispered.

Dying.

"Shh." He uncrossed his legs and stretched out a little farther, his erection pulsing so intensely he was afraid he would burst. "Okay, now, point your fingertips toward the floor. Yes…that's it. Now, every so slowly, slowly…slide them toward the hem of your shorts."

The very short, very decadent edge of her frayed denim shorts that barely covered her sweet bottom when she bent over.

But that description was solely for him as he slid his hand under the flap of the towel and wrapped his fingers around the base of his straining erection.

"Okay," she whispered, so low it could have been a sigh.

"Okay, then…" Where was he? Oh, yes. Her shorts. "I want you to let your fingertips drift over the edge of the hem so that they're touching your leg. Yes, that's it."

Somewhere down the line it had ceased being him guiding her hand over her body. In his mind, it had become his hand.

"Mmm. Now...curl your fingers under the hem. Don't tug the material away. Rather keep your knuckles against your skin. Yes, that's it. Now move your hand toward your inner thigh. Slowly. Very slowly."

He heard her labored breathing over the phone and closed his eyes. Oh, sweet torture.

"Now, straighten your fingers so that the very tips are at the edge of your panties..."

"I'm not—"

"Shh."

God, she wasn't wearing underwear? That little piece of information nearly sent him sailing right over the edge.

"Move your fingers, just the tips, until they're touching your curls. Tell me how they feel."

He heard her swallow hard. "I thought I wasn't supposed to talk."

"Except when I ask you to."

"Oh." Silence, then, "They're wiry...yet soft. Hot and so very, very wet..."

"Mmm." Sam tightened his hand around his pulsing arousal, feeling the heat and dampness from his own reaction. "Now, slowly, ever so slowly, inch your fingers toward the source of that wetness. That's it. Don't rush it. Feel that tightness in your belly? The thick beating of your heart? The hypersensitivity of your nipples? Run the pad of your index finger over the bit of flesh at the apex. Mmm."

"Oh, yes!" Layla's breath rushed out.

"Oh, no. Not yet, Layla. I'm not through with you yet. Hold on with me, baby. Hold on."

Long moments passed with neither of them saying anything, then Sam voiced his final direction, "Now take off your shorts." He waited a few beats then continued. "I want you to slide your finger the length of your swollen flesh, right through the shallow channel. Are you doing it? That's it. Back and forth…back and forth…"

He had to release his own hold to keep from coming.

"Now, part your folds with your thumb and middle finger. Mmm. Yes. Feel the cool air caressing you there? Now find your entrance with your index finger and lightly rub there. Yes, that's it. Right, there…"

Sam's muscles virtually shook with the need to release himself.

"Now, slide that finger where it so wants to go, baby. Do it for us. Do it for me…"

Layla's sharp cry filled his ear, and he grasped tightly onto his erection, sliding his hand up and down until his own desire for her spilled out.

"Holy shit," he murmured long moments later. "I don't think I've ever had such a powerful orgasm without somebody else in the room."

He heard her moving around. "Thanks, Sam," she whispered. "Good night."

"Wait!"

But she had already hung up.

He stared at the cordless receiver for a long moment, then pressed the disconnect button.

"Well, how do you like that for wham-bam, thank you ma'am?" he said to the empty room.

But even as he said the words, his grin was wide and languid and he felt...well, unlike any other way he'd ever felt before.

And he couldn't wait until he'd finally proved whatever it was he was trying to prove, and their virtual sex could revert back to the pure, mind-blowing real thing.

He tossed the phone to the sofa beside him then pushed himself to his feet with some effort.

It looked like another shower was in order. But he intended to take his time. After all, he had to exorcise all those images of Layla touching herself in the middle of her bedroom. And for the first time since he was a teenager he found he looked forward to the experience.

Especially when he found himself wondering if she was doing the same thing across town...

10

THE FOLLOWING Monday morning Layla was still mortified by what had happened Saturday night. Coming into work at the center, she navigated the halls as if she was on a covert mission. What she was really doing was avoiding any accidental meetings with Sam, afraid her embarrassment would be obvious from the ceaseless burning of her face.

Which was ridiculous, really. She was a grown woman, after all, and phone sex was sex. Consensual sex between her and a very willing man. A man who had easily persuaded her to throw caution to the wind and indulge in one of her most wicked fantasies.

Then she'd had that incredible orgasm, hung up on him, and within five minutes had turned into a total basket case.

What if someone had seen her?

What if Sam told anyone what had happened?

What if Sam looked at her differently?

"You're a moron," she said to herself, writing a note on the chart from her last patient then plopping the folder down on the pile of others in her out-box.

"Pardon me?" said Traci Bangs, the receptionist she shared with two other doctors.

Layla stared at her where she stood in the door. "I wasn't talking to you. I was talking to me."

"Oh. Then I suppose it's okay." Traci smiled and put a handful of messages on her desk. "He called three more times."

Layla crumpled the top three messages and tossed them into the garbage can one by one. "He who?"

Traci wrinkled her face in a frown that said, "Do you think I was born yesterday?"

Great. That's just what she needed on top of everything else. More gossip at the center about her and a colleague. And not just any colleague but the staff administrator, her boss. No, he might not be married, but that didn't make the situation any easier. Being intimately linked to anyone at the center was akin to professional suicide. She'd learned that the hard way. You couldn't go to a meeting without everyone in the room looking at you speculatively, a long, awkward moment ensuing where no one knew what to say and the meeting's agenda flying straight out the window.

And forget it if you were seen with the person. No matter how innocuous the meeting, by the time that piece of gossip made the rounds, the two of you had been going at it hot and heavy in an empty examining room, wild animal noises filling the hallway outside.

"Are you okay, Dr. Hollister?" Traci asked.

Layla hadn't realized she was still in the room. "Please, call me Layla," she said for the millionth time since Traci had been hired on a year before. "And aside from feeling like jumping out the closest window, I'm fine."

Oh, that was subtle. She could only imagine what the rumor mill would make of that little remark. *Staff Administrative Hunk Dumps Underling, Inspiring Suicidal Thoughts. Suicide Watch in Effect Until Further Notice.*

Traci blinked at her.

"I'm fine," she said with a forced smile. "Should Dr. Lovejoy—" she shivered "—call again, put him right through, even if I'm with a patient."

Traci smiled and sighed in a strange way. "Will do."

Layla watched her leave, wondering what the sigh was about.

She pulled her next patient file forward, noting that the appointment wasn't for another twenty minutes. She glanced at her watch. Just enough time for her to run to the bathroom and splash some cold water on her still-burning face.

She gathered her purse from her drawer and rounded her desk, only to be thrown another curve in the shape of her father.

Oh, boy, the day just kept getting better and better.

"Dad," she said, growing even more flustered. "What a surprise."

His chuckle was low and warm as he kissed her on the cheek and waited for her to do the same to him. "I hope I haven't caught you at a bad time, Elizabeth. I had breakfast with an old colleague of mine in cardio and thought I'd come back with him so I could say hello."

"No, of course it's not a bad time. I mean, I welcome a visit from you anytime."

He eyed her. "Are you coming down with something? You look a little feverish."

Marvelous. Now her father was noticing her embarrassed flush. "No, no. I'm fine. Just been a little hectic around here this morning, that's all."

"Oh? Bart told me that you're a little on the low side with patient load."

Bart being Bartholomew Macmillan, one of the senior board members.

Great, just great.

Layla stared at her father as if he were an alien just dropped from space. "Pardon me?"

"Hmm. I take it you haven't been approached about this subject yet?"

Approached...by whom?

Oh.

By Dr. Sam Lovejoy, of course.

She ignored the shiver.

"Um, no, I can't say as I have." She forced another smile. "But thank you for the heads-up."

"Glad I could help."

He could help her by holding the window open for her while she jumped.

Here she had been avoiding Sam's calls all morning thinking he wanted to talk about their...intimate behavior Saturday night, and instead he'd likely been trying to set up a meeting with her to discuss Center business.

She briefly mashed her eyes shut. Could this morning possibly get any worse?

"Well, good morning, Dr. Hollister. Or should I say Drs. Hollister?"

Layla opened her eyes. Her question had just been answered in the form of a grinning Sam Lovejoy.

WAS IT HIM or did Layla look a little flushed this morning?

Sam shook hands with the preeminent medical researcher Dr. Thomas Hollister, having met him a couple of years ago at some charity function or another and crossed paths with him several times at other functions over the years.

That's it. That was the reason why Layla's color was high and why she had been avoiding him. She'd been sick. Had probably spent all day yesterday in bed fighting off a fever or a virus or something while he'd envisioned her staring at the answering machine as he left message after message.

The problem was that combining the words *Layla* and *bed* brought forth all sorts of wicked, inappropriate images. Especially inappropriate considering he was talking to her father.

"You two know each other?" Layla asked. Then she sighed and held up her hand. "Forget I asked that question. Of course, you know each other. You move in the same circles, don't you?"

She'd said *circles* in the same tone one would use to describe the color of phlegm. Sam frowned at her. Just what in the hell was that supposed to mean?

"Sam and I have met on several occasions," Thomas said. "But I do have to say it's a pleasure running into you here. I don't believe I've had a chance to congratulate you on your new position with the Center."

"Thank you, sir. I appreciate the sentiment."

Sam looked from father to daughter, noticing a tension there that surprised him. Of course, when Layla had told him about her upbringing, and he'd glimpsed the picture taken over a decade ago, he hadn't immediately put together that the father she hadn't known until she was a teenager was *the* Dr. Thomas Hollister. But now that he had…well, the information morphed into much more.

"You know, this accidental meeting gives me the opportunity to do something I've been meaning to do for some time now," Thomas said. "Why don't you join us—and by 'us' I mean my dear wife Sharon and my daughter Elizabeth—for dinner this coming Sunday afternoon? It will give us a chance to get to know each other better."

Elizabeth? Who was Elizabeth? Then he saw the way Thomas woodenly put his arm around Layla and knew he was referring to her.

"I'm sure Dr. Lovejoy would agree this is awfully last-minute, Father," she said.

"Nonsense. We'll expect you at one o'clock sharp, Elizabeth." He then kissed Layla's cheek, shook Sam's hand and walked confidently down the hall without a second glance.

Sam exhaled. "Well…"

Layla grabbed him by the arm and led him to the nearest empty examining room where she closed and locked the door behind them.

Sam hiked a brow at her.

"What was all that about?" she hissed.

"What was all what about?" he asked, knowing damn well what she was talking about as he opened the lid of a glass jar and fished out a tongue depressor. "I was invited to dinner and I accepted."

"By my father."

"By the best friend of the chairman of the board, so to speak." He waggled the depressor at her. "Care to play doctor?"

"Sure. Hop up on the examining table and I'll perform a rectal exam."

"Ouch." Sam abandoned the depressor. "Not quite what I had in mind."

"So tell me what you did have in mind when you decided to drop by my office, Sam?" she said, crossing her arms in a way that made him think *uh-*

oh. "No, wait a minute. Could it be to set up a meeting to discuss my disappointing patient load?"

Definitely *uh-oh.* He forced himself to stop fiddling with the materials on the counter and face her. "I came by to see why you've been avoiding me for the past day and a half." The redness he'd noticed in her face earlier returned full-flush. "I even came to your apartment last night and you pretended you weren't there."

"Maybe I wasn't."

"Your car was parked on the street and I heard the television before I knocked."

"Maybe I was on a date."

He stared at her.

"Okay, maybe I wasn't on a date. But I was watching *The Bachelor.* And no one comes between me and *The Bachelor.*"

"And here I thought I was the only bachelor you were interested in."

"That's because you're cocky."

"Yeah, well, at least I'm honest."

"What's that supposed to mean?"

He crossed his arms to counter her stance even though he couldn't help grinning. "Admit it, Hollister, you're ashamed of what happened the other night."

He swore she almost turned purple. "I am not."

"My point exactly."

She dropped her arms to her sides and curled her hands into fists. "What are you talking about? And what is it with everyone and they're damn points lately? First I have Mallory telling me stuff that doesn't make any sense and now you're standing in the middle of my examining room referring to a conversation that we never had.''

''The honesty point. That's the point I'm making. I—'' he jabbed his thumb into his chest ''—am being honest in saying I thoroughly enjoyed what passed between us the other night. You...'' he slowly crossed the room until he had her backed up against the door, then poked his finger into her chest ''...are pretending it never happened.''

''You couldn't be further from the truth.''

''Oh?'' He leaned closer yet, until he could softly blow on the flushed skin of her neck. ''So tell me then, Dr. Hollister,'' he murmured, breathing in her unique scent, ''did you reach climax?''

He heard her swallow deeply, but his attention was on the curve of her ear and the tiny gold earring she wore. ''I don't know what you're talking about.''

''Bingo.''

''No go,'' she said, but her voice had dropped to a whisper.

''Tsk, tsk.'' He was afraid if he touched her, he wouldn't be able to stop, so he limited himself to fingering a stray strand of her hair. ''Lie to yourself all you want, Layla. But I know the truth.''

He stood like that for a long moment, not really

touching her, but closer than any casual conversation dictated.

"Well, then," she said, her voice catching in that telltale way that drove him nuts, "as long as we're being truthful, suppose you explain to me why you stopped having sex with me?"

"We had sex Saturday night."

She made a throaty sound of frustration.

"And we're having sex tonight."

"I won't answer my phone."

"It's not your phone I'll be calling on, Layla."

She pulled back slightly to look at him, forcing the back of her head against the door. She stared into his eyes. "You mean...?"

He nodded. "Oh, yeah. Full-out penetration."

She shivered.

He grinned.

And someone knocked on the door.

Layla nearly jumped out of her skin. Sam merely walked over to it and called, "Come back in five."

A muffled female voice said words neither of them could make out then retreated.

Layla collapsed against the door, but this time it had nothing to do with his nearness. "Oh, that's going to give the gossip mill all sorts of raw material to work with."

Sam chuckled, leaving his hand against the door and blocking her escape with his body. "Is that really what you're worried about, Layla?"

"Actually, I'm more worried about the discussion

going on behind my back about my low patient load.''

"Mmm. Official stuff. I'm not ready to move onto that yet. Not when I have a wet and wicked woman in my arms.''

"I'm not wet...'' She allowed her words to drift off, likely because she knew all too well that there was a way to verify that information and Sam wouldn't hesitate to use it.

"So...'' he began. "Your place at, say, ten-thirty?''

She stared at him, so sexily exasperated that he wanted to check out her wetness anyway.

"Make it closer to eleven,'' she said.

AND TO THINK, just a few short hours ago she'd felt ashamed at some harmless phone sex.

Layla stretched her arms above her head, her legs tangled with Sam's across her bed. Her head was near the foot while his was off to the side near the headboard. She tried to remember how they got to be in that position then blew her hair from her eyes and smiled. It didn't really matter, did it? Because what they'd done in the past three hours far surpassed anything she'd been expecting.

"I swear, you're going to kill me,'' Sam murmured, still out of breath.

"Latent cardio problems, Dr. Lovejoy?'' She shivered again on top of the aftershocks from her last climax.

"No, but no man can be healthy enough to take this kind of abuse." She felt his hand on her calf, his fingers squeezing then running up the length of her inner thigh. "You're an insatiable wench."

"So what does that make you?"

"Oh, I don't know. Horny toad should about cover it."

She laughed, shuddering when his fingers touched her. She rolled away from him and repositioned herself so they were lying side by side. "You know, Sam, you never did explain to me the reason behind the dry spell."

He had his arm bent over his eyes. "Mmm."

She prodded him. "Oh, no, I'm not about to let you get away with ducking the question again."

"Tell me why you don't want me to go to dinner at your father's house and I'll tell you why."

Layla made a face. "What is it with you and conditions?"

She watched his mouth curve into a grin. "There wouldn't be conditions if you just came out and answered my questions."

"While I get nothing in return for mine."

Layla's muscles refused to pull together for battle. Instead she lay boneless against her crisp white sheets and wondered what she was doing in bed with a guy who exasperated her beyond belief. She turned her head and smiled into her pillow away from him. Oh, yeah. The incredible sex.

Then he said, "I was afraid the sex would turn."

Layla turned her head back around to look at him, then had to swipe her hair from her eyes. "What?"

Sam peeked out from under his arm. "It's been my experience that when something starts that hot and heavy, it can't help but burn out quickly. One week and—*bam!*—nothing but ashes." He put his arm back over his face. "That and a lot of wondering what you'd been thinking 'cause you're not attracted to the person at all anymore."

Layla thought about that one for a long moment. "I don't know if I should feel insulted that I rate so closely to other women you've dated, flattered that I turn you on that much, or afraid that tomorrow I'll see you and you'll look at me like you don't know who I am."

He didn't answer.

She dragged the pillow out from under her head and hit him with it.

He lifted up on his elbows, his hair sexily tousled. "What?"

"Did you hear what I said?"

He grinned. "Yeah, I heard you."

"And?"

"And...well..."

She felt like shoving him out of her bed.

"I think you should stick with flattered, Dr. Hollister. Because what I feel with you? Well, I'm beginning to think it just might be fueled by a source that isn't going to run out anytime soon."

She made a face. "But you think it will."

"I'm holding off judgment."

"My ass." She began to get out of bed.

"Your sweet ass." He reached out and gave her bottom a squeeze. She swatted his hand away.

"Is that what you were really thinking? That you didn't want to have sex because you were afraid you were going to wake up in the morning and wonder what you were doing with me?"

His grimace was almost endearing. Almost. If only she didn't want to bash him in the face a few more times with her pillow.

"Not me, so much. My sister...well, never mind. Anyway, the way I see it, you should be flattered."

"And you should be flattened."

"No, wait," he said, when she started to get up. "You're missing the point here."

She stared at him.

"Okay, forget the point. You're missing what I was trying to say. I didn't want what was developing between us to burn out. To go the way so many relationships have gone before. You were special and I...well, I want it to last."

"A little longer anyway, huh?"

He ran his fingertips down her back over her cotton camisole. "A lot longer."

She looked at him over her shoulder. "How much longer?"

He cracked one of his cocky grins and she braced herself for his answer. "At least until the charity ball. You know how hard it is to get a date on such short notice?''

She reached for the pillow to bean him again, but he caught it and tackled her back to the bed. He reached over to switch on the light. Layla blinked, thinking that her makeup was probably smeared all over her face and that her hair was probably sticking up at all kinds of strange angles.

''Now, don't you think it's time you showed me what you've been hiding in the dark?''

Oh, she'd forgotten that little detail. The fact that her chest was as flat as the Mojave Desert.

He tugged on the hem of her camisole and she held it down.

He raised his brows, looking like temptation incarnate with his hair flopping over his eyes in that sexy way. ''You're kidding me, right?''

''I am *so* not kidding you.''

He made a face. ''You do know that I've made a living out of seeing women's breasts.''

''Thanks for the reminder. I'd forgotten.''

He tried to go in from the top. She compensated. ''Layla…''

''Sam…'' she said in the same warning tone.

He put his hands on either side of her head and kissed her senseless. ''Give me a date.''

She blinked at him and licked her lips restlessly, wanting more of his kisses. ''What?''

''A date for the unveiling. You know, the night when you voluntarily reveal all.''

"Okay…never."

"That's not a date."

"December 12, 3010."

"Won't matter, we'll both be skeletons."

"Exactly."

He twirled a strand of her hair around and around his index finger. "I don't know why you're making such a big deal out of this. I mean, I've seen everything else." He waggled his brows at her. "Several times. In fact, I'm becoming very well acquainted with every curve, opening and orifice."

She couldn't help herself. She laughed. "I'm not the one making a big deal out of it. You are."

"So you think it's natural that a guy's girl doesn't want him to see her breasts in the light?"

"Soon," she said.

His grin widened. "That's more like it." He slid his hand between their bodies, then edged it down so he could nudge apart her thighs. "Now, where were we, exactly…?"

11

THE WEEK whizzed by in a blur of work and sex.
Layla tried to tell herself she didn't have the time
to try to figure out what exactly Sam had meant by
his temporary moratorium on sex. Besides, he hadn't
done it again. The routine was, she'd work at the
center during the day, the clinic at night, and by
eleven o'clock she and Sam were in her bed. If anything, the passion that existed between them was
spiraling higher and higher until she could almost
come with one look from him.

This was unusual for a woman who usually
couldn't even achieve orgasm until at least the third
time with a man. Now she had so many a night she
couldn't keep track of them.

But as she checked in at the clinic before going
home to get ready for the stupid charity event she'd
promised Sam she'd attend with him, she couldn't
help but think about the meaning behind his words.

Did he expect to wake up one morning and find
his desire for her had vanished?

And how about her? Had she even stopped long
enough to take a breath, much less considered where

all of this could be leading, except toward a very bad breakup?

Of course a breakup usually meant one had to be going out. And up until now she and Sam really hadn't done that, had they? They couldn't seem to stay out of bed long enough to do anything. Except last Saturday when he'd met Mallory, Reilly and Jack at her place. But that didn't really count because there had been no invitation offered or accepted.

She felt like banging her head against her office door. Instead she opened it—and ran straight into Lupe.

"You look like hell," the nurse said, giving her a good once-over.

Definitely not what she needed to hear an hour and half before Sam was due to pick her up at her apartment for what would probably be a long, exhausting night. "A woman after my own heart."

Lupe smiled and shrugged. "Just thought I'd tell you the truth. 'Cause it doesn't look like anyone else is going to do it."

Layla frowned at her. "How do you mean?"

Had Lupe somehow heard through the medical grapevine that all was not as it seemed between her and Sam? Was there something she didn't know? Damn the rumor mill. Every now and again important information ran through it that one of the parties involved had no knowledge of.

Like Jim Colton's being and staying married.

Lupe shrugged again, then folded her arms over her ample chest. "Just that I don't think the board that runs this clinic is being straight with us." She lifted a finger. "Just last week two more clinics were closed down. Lack of funds, they said. Our patient load gets higher and the funds get lower." She shook her head. "Makes no sense."

"But we're waiting for them to assign us another doctor."

Lupe snorted. "And I believe in the tooth fairy."

Layla stared at the other woman. Was it true? Were they at risk of being closed down? She already put so much time in at the clinic she could barely function from lack of sleep. She ignored the fact that lately Sam played a part in that, because she deserved at least that much of a personal life. Despite the hours she worked, her new patient load had sharply increased with more and more families facing layoffs and the economy not looking as though it would turn around anytime soon.

She looked out into the waiting room. The majority of the patients there Lupe could look after. The others who needed further medical attention would be referred to the L.A. County Hospital.

Lupe looked just as concerned as she felt, but she managed a smile. "But never mind that now. You have a date tonight, no?" She helped Layla to shrug out of her lab coat then gave her a shove toward the door. "Go. Go have fun. The clinic will still be here tomorrow."

And so would their problems and their limitless patients.

Layla suddenly felt dizzy with it all.

"Go and eat caviar and drink Dom DeLuise so you can come in tomorrow morning and tell me all about it."

Layla laughed. "You know it's—"

"Yeah, I know. I read the star sheets just the same as you. Now go."

And Layla went.

THERE was one thing Sam was absolutely sure of. And that was Dr. Layla Hollister didn't have a clue how hot she really was.

He paused for a moment with two champagne flutes in his hands, awestruck by the modest cut of her deep-purple dress that looked anything but modest on her tall, slender frame. From the elegant curve of her neck and shoulders with her dark hair piled up on top of her head, to the roundness of her perfect bottom, she naturally outshone other women in the room who'd paid a fortune for their curves.

He should know. He'd been the one they paid. And it wasn't that he didn't do good work. It was just that Layla radiated a beauty that couldn't be bought, borrowed or stolen. Even though she hated being there and looked at her watchless wrist countless times, she always had a friendly smile for passersby. She was completely oblivious that most of those passersby were men and that they'd gone by once or twice apparently trying to muster the courage to talk to her.

He remembered thinking she was a model when they'd first met and imagined that others probably thought that as well. And if he didn't hurry back, he might have to stand in line to talk to his own date.

"Beat it, Buster, she's mine," he said as he came up behind someone who had found the wherewithal to talk to her.

The man sputtered a couple of times then moved away.

Layla nearly choked as she laughed. "I can't believe you just did that! 'Beat it, Buster'?"

He shook his head. "His name is Buster and he works in toxicology at UCLA Med." He handed her a flute. "And he's also just announced his engagement to wife number three and has five kids split between the other two."

"Yikes."

"Yikes is right."

"Right at home here in L.A. then." She squinted at him. "What would you say the average marriage rate is?"

"Including or excluding J.Lo?"

She rolled her eyes.

"Too many to think about," he said, downing half his champagne without even realizing he was doing it.

Truth was, he always felt a little…antsy when talk turned to marriage. It's not that he had anything against it. It wasn't like he had a plaque over his bed that read Bachelor Forever or anything. It was just that he hadn't given it a whole lot of thought. At least not seriously.

Except for recently.

But of course that was because he'd just received a handwritten invitation from Heather announcing her wedding in a month to Brian the Jerk.

A top-heavy woman in a tight red sequinned dress sashayed by, wearing a big smile. Sam smiled back.

Layla rolled her eyes.

"What?" he asked.

"Nothing. It's just that I would feel a little more comfortable if you didn't look like a starving man in front of an open buffet."

He grinned. "Baby, the only food I'm interested in eating is you." He waggled his brows.

She laughed then sipped her champagne.

"And my attention in the other women in the room isn't what you might think."

"Oh? I suppose you'd smile that way at them if they were male, as well."

"Hmm. Probably not."

"Hmm. Didn't think so."

She was jealous. As jealous as he'd been when he'd come upon Buster making his sleazy move. "You see, I wasn't looking at that woman for normal mating purposes."

She nearly spat her champagne over his custom-tailored tux.

"Oh, no. I was trying to place her. And I smiled when I had. February 2002. Breast enlargement, tummy tuck and butt implants."

Layla's brows rose as she tried to track down the woman in question.

He shrugged. "She was also Miss August."

She made a face. "You probably have the centerfold pasted up on your wall."

"Mmm. Actually, I do. Signed, no less. And it hangs with at least a dozen others in the waiting room." He moved his glass to his other hand and lightly touched her lower back to lead her toward the dining room. "Well, I should say they were hung in the waiting room of my old office. Now that I'm an important staff administrator at an important institution...well, I don't have time for breasts and stuff."

"Liar."

He chuckled. "Beyond your breasts, that is." He was behind her and discreetly moved so that he was flush up against her back. He whispered into her ear, "And you still haven't told me when the big unveiling is going to be."

"As soon as you stop asking, I'll start showing."

"Oh. Forget I asked." He urged her toward the buffet. "Eat."

"In this dress? Forget it."

Another slinky female with excellent ta-tas happened by. He couldn't place her. Must be one of Hanlan's.

"You know," Layla said, filling a small gold-edged plate with finger foods. "I'd feel better if I didn't know you've not only seen the majority of the female guests' breasts, but that you probably worked on them, too." She made a face. "Gives a whole new meaning to Silicon, or rather Silicone, Valley."

"Saline."

She stared at him.

"The implants are all saline now."

"I know that, doofus."

"Oh."

She looked at her bare wrist again. "How long did you say we have to stay here?"

"Your decision, babycakes."

"If it were my decision we wouldn't be here."

"Sam!"

He instantly recognized Bartholomew Macmillan's voice. Layla gave him an exasperated look as the older man and senior board member of the Center descended on them, his wife in tow. Introductions were made, then Bart's wife, Deirdre, said, "Dr. Hollister and I are already acquainted, my dear. She's on staff at one of the free clinics I administer."

And so it went. As Bart motioned him toward the room where many of the old boys' network were enjoying cognac and cigars, Sam watched Deirdre take Layla's arm and lead her toward the balcony doors.

Why did he suddenly have the feeling that they would be staying at the party longer than even he had planned?

"BREASTS, breasts, breasts. Everywhere you looked there were these..."

"Let me guess," Mallory said to Layla the following morning at Mallory's apartment near Sunset Boulevard. "Breasts."

Layla wasn't entirely certain why she'd felt compelled to seek out her friend so early on a Saturday morning. Especially since Sam was still handsomely asleep in her bed and she was due at the clinic in an hour. But here she was, choking back instant cappuccino and wishing she'd thought to stop at Reilly's shop to pick up some sticky buns and coffee.

Layla laughed. "There's probably a law somewhere limiting the number of times you can say breasts in one sentence."

"If so, then you broke it at least three times." Mallory collected the newspapers scattered around the tiny kitchen table and dropped them onto the cluttered floor. "Anyway, it's probably only illegal in Alabama or South Carolina or somewhere. We're in L.A." She tilted her dark head. "Or had you forgotten?"

Layla made a face, reflecting her feelings not only

about her friend's observation but about the coffee she was trying to drink. "No."

"Looks like that's not the only thing you've forgotten."

Layla looked at her.

"You seemed to have conveniently pushed aside that Dr. Lovejoy there, no matter how yummy and how good a poker player he is, is a tit-face-and-butt man."

Layla rolled her eyes. "I have not forgotten."

"Oh, yes, you have. Why else would it have bothered you so much last night?"

"Oh, I don't know. Because it's the first time we've actually been out anywhere in public together, maybe?"

A thump sounded from the other room.

Layla looked in the direction of the bedroom. The door was closed, which wasn't all that surprising since Mallory usually kept her bedroom door closed, if just to hide what a messy person she was.

"What was that?"

"What was what?" Mallory asked, looking at her deadpan.

"That thump, that's what."

"What thump?"

Layla looked at her friend more closely. Sure, she figured she'd dragged Mallory out of bed this early. And her faded blue T-shirt, plaid pajama boxers and tangled hair told her that was the case. What she hadn't expected was that Mallory had been with somebody else in that bed.

Mallory looked down at her T-shirt with the words PETA—People for the Eating of Tasty Animals written across the chest. "A smartass gift from someone I worked with," she said. "I should have burned it when I got it."

Layla stared at her, Mall's T-shirt the furthest thing from her mind and they both knew it. "Hmm. Okay, either you own up to knowing what the thump was or I'm dialing 911," she said levelly.

While their places were similarly cramped, Layla's was in a slightly better part of town where she didn't have to worry about chasing icky bugs across the wall with a shoe. Mallory's place, on the other hand, was in the seediest of seedy areas and her neighbors made no secret of being prostitutes and other shady characters Layla got the chills just walking by.

Layla reached into her purse to take out her cell phone.

Mallory's shoulders slumped. "I know what the thump was." She held up a hand. "But don't ask me to share the source of it, because it's not at sharing stage yet."

"Not at sharing stage yet?" Layla gave up on the coffee and pushed it away. "I tell you from stage one about Sam, even knowing how you're going to react, and you're not even going to tell me who's in the other room?"

"You only told me about Sam because you were hoping I'd talk you out of it."

"Maybe. But that doesn't change the fact that I'm sitting in your apartment and there could be a serial killer in the next room listening to every word I'm saying."

Mallory rolled her eyes. "He's not a serial killer."

"Well, at least we established it's a man."

Mallory crossed her legs up on her chair. "What's that supposed to mean?"

Layla shrugged. "Oh, I don't know. You've gone without for so long that Reilly and I were beginning to wonder if you'd switched sides."

"If I had, you don't think you and Reilly would be the ones I'd hit on first?" Mallory winked at her.

Layla leveled a gaze at her. "You've been living in this neighborhood too long." Her eyes slowly widened. "That…he…the guy in the other room isn't one of your neighbors, is he?"

"No, of course not. I mean, it would be okay if he were. Far be it from me to judge a guy by his product, but it's not."

"Judge a guy by his product? Mallory, the product in question is drugs."

"And I just told you that he's not a dealer."

"Oh. Sorry. I got caught up on the one detail." She glanced at her watch, happy to find it right where she wanted it. Last night she'd gone insane not knowing what time it was. "God, I've got to go."

"I'm sorry to hear that," Mallory said with a bright smile.

"You...me...we need to powwow. Soon."

"Uh-huh. Just as soon as we get your mess figured out."

"What I have is not a mess."

"Uh-huh. That's why you keep seeking me out hoping I'll talk you out of it."

"Oh, sometimes I hate that you know me so well."

"So does this mean I failed? To talk you out of it?"

"Sadly, yes." Layla slung her purse over her shoulder then held it closely to her side. You never knew who was lurking outside Mall's apartment. Hell, you didn't know who lurked inside it.

"Oh, and Mall?"

She found her friend on her heels, her attention on the closed bedroom door. "Hmm?" She turned to look at her.

"You need anything, and I mean anything, you know where I'm at."

Mallory smiled at her, genuinely this time. "Yeah, I know. Thanks."

12

LATER that night Layla padded from the bathroom to her bedroom where Sam was stretched across the tangled sheets, his glorious chest glistening with sweat from the sex they'd had. She'd put her panties back on, and since she still had on her black camisole, she supposed she was fully covered. As usual, Sam had his arm draped over his eyes. It seemed to be some sort of ritual with him. Block out the world until he was ready to make sense of it again.

She switched on the lamp. He moved his arm and peeked out at her. Layla grabbed the bottom of her camisole then quickly lifted it, flashing him before shoving the material back down again.

"Oh, no, wait! I wasn't ready," Sam complained, jackknifing into a sitting position.

"Too bad."

He stared at her in challenge. "Too bad, huh? What remains is too bad for whom."

He flipped her onto her back across the foot of the bed. "Hey! No fair."

"And you call what you just did fair? Hell, the flasher down on Sunset gives you a better look than you just gave me."

"Then go down to Sunset."

"Sorry, but it's not his breasts I'm interested in."

"Too bad."

He flattened his hand against her bare belly then slid it upward, his palm searing her skin as he edged under her camisole. She merely stared up at him, wondering if he'd dare go to the next stage. A part of her was afraid he would. Another part wanted him to take the decision out of her hands. This had gone on too long. Her initial neurotic reaction to his wanting to see her in the light had ballooned into something altogether different. And uncomfortable. And she just wanted it over with.

But Sam didn't appear to feel the same way as he caressed her breasts under cover for a long moment, then dropped his mouth to encircle her right nipple through the warm silk.

"You know," he said moments later, after she got all hot and bothered. "That would feel a whole lot better without the material between us."

Layla yanked her top off in one move, then lay back.

Strangely enough, she found she was tense. What would he say, this doctor of breasts? Would he evaluate her? Would he find her wanting?

His grin told her no. And when he leaned forward to run his tongue the length of her nipple, she forgot all about the thought.

"Now that's more like it," he said, suckling the sensitive flesh in the light from the lamp even as he caressed her other breast with his hand. "God, I can't tell you how often I dreamed about just this moment."

"You're not disappointed?" Lord knew she was. She was a small B at best, a high A at worst. And when she lay down all that existed were two pointy nipples that seemed way too big.

"What's there to be disappointed about, Layla? You're beautiful," he rasped.

And in that moment, as he laved her and stroked her, she felt that way. Beautiful, desirable...and so hot she wanted him again, even though they'd just spent the past two hours setting the sheets on fire.

Layla caught Sam's shoulders and rolled him over until she was straddling him. Some gymnastics were called for to get out of her panties, but once they were off, she reached for the light.

He caught her hand, quiet for a long moment. Then said, "Leave it on."

His eyes twinkled at her suggestively, not quite a dare, but not quite *not* a dare.

She itched to plunge the room back into darkness. To lose herself in sensation and forget the world existed. And it was easier to do that with the lights off.

She quickly sheathed him then positioned herself over his pulsing arousal, pausing for effect—and to allow her to reach for the lamp again.

Sam's hips bucked up to meet her, thrusting deep into her body, making the hand that was reaching for the light stop short and grab hold of the head-board to steady herself.

There was nothing she wouldn't grant him when he filled her like that. And that was the word, too. *Filled.* He filled her senses with his very essence every time they had sex. He filled her heart with longing and passion. He filled her physically almost to the point of pain, yet gave her the purest of all pleasures.

Layla tilted her hips forward, then leaned forward, trying to rub her bare breasts against his chest. He held her upright with his hands on her hips, his eyes watchful, shifting to take in her neck, her breasts, then where they were joined.

He groaned.

Poker-sharp heat built deep in her belly as she moved up and down his long, thick shaft. She remembered his words from the previous Saturday. *Slowly, slowly.* There was no need to rush. They'd already done enough of that. Now it was time to draw out the sensations, the emotions, revel in the uniqueness of them.

She stretched her neck, a soul-deep moan floating from her throat as he pressed his hot palms against her nipples then pinched the tips, sending red shafts of heat down to her groin.

Sam made a sound between a groan and growl as he shifted her off him then turned her so she was on her hands and knees. He positioned himself behind her and reentered with a long, hard stroke, hitting her G-spot dead on then stroking it until Layla shivered from the need for release.

"Oh, please, please, please," she whispered, a droplet of sweat rolling down the side of her face. She bunched the sheets in her hands then laid her head down against the mattress to allow for deeper penetration. He took her cue and adjusted his stroke, hitting deeper and farther and faster, until the erotic slap of flesh against flesh filled her ears, sweat coated her skin and the best damn orgasm of her life ripped through her body.

GO FIGURE. The sex just keeps getting better and better.

Sam lay flat on his back, trying to catch his breath as Layla lay on her stomach, her head lolling over the side of the mattress at an angle, her dark hair nearly hiding her face.

Whoa. He draped his arm over his eyes. Was there such a thing as having too much great sex? Could a person actually be sexed to death? While he couldn't recall seeing any headlines touting such an event, he also didn't think that kind of news was the type newspapers were likely to highlight. Up-and-Coming Plastic Surgeon Comes to Death. No, he didn't think reports of that nature made the front page of the *Los Angeles Times*. But the rag sheets Layla loved to read would probably have a piece as raunchy as that as their first feature.

Dozens of augmented mourners filed past the coffin today, wondering which high profile L.A. plastic surgeon was going to see to their next enlargement/reduction/nip/tuck/lipo/implant procedure now that Dr. Lovejoy has bitten the dust.

Sam grinned at the lunacy of his own thoughts, his heart rate finally beginning to slow, his breathing manageable. His other hand absently slid across the back of Layla's bare knee. What was it about this one woman that made him want her so much? Morning, noon and night there she was, in the creases of his consciousness, her soft laugh, her supple body, her saucy smile, her smartass remarks. He went to the market and at the checkout stand he thought of her as he glanced at the front page of those idiotic scandal sheets. During a work-related dinner he would stare at his glass of club soda and remember the night they'd met. Every time he went into his house, he vividly recalled both occasions they'd had sex on his couch. The first when she was physically there, the second…

His grin widened.

"God, sometimes I wish I could crawl inside your head and have a look around," Layla mumbled.

Sam rubbed his brows with his arm then covered his closed eyes again. "No, you don't."

A long pause, then, "Yeah, you're right. I probably wouldn't like what I saw."

She made a move to get up, but he held her leg to the mattress. "Oh, I don't know. I think you'd get a big head if you knew how much I thought about you."

"Yeah?"

"Oh, yeah."

"Hmm. Good thing I can't read your thoughts, then, because your head is big enough for the both of us."

Sam grinned.

"Anyway, since we've both decided that my crawling inside your head is not the way to go, you're going to have to tell me what's on your mind. You seem in, um, pretty good spirits now, but when you first got here you seemed distracted."

"Mmm." He was reluctant to shift out of his current mood.

"Did something happen at work?" she asked softly.

Sam made a face. "What is it with women and their questions?"

She lightly knocked her loose fist against his leg.

He drew in a deep breath, actually relieved that she'd noticed the change in his demeanor. Truth was, he had been distracted. Majorly so.

"I got a wedding invitation from my sister yesterday," he murmured.

Her hand stilled on his leg. "That's nice. Why would that preoccupy you?"

"Maybe because I don't want her to marry the moron she's picked as a mate?"

A soft sound that could have been laughter. "Well, I can certainly see where that might throw a monkey wrench into the mix."

"Monkey wrench?"

"You know what I mean."

He grinned. Yeah, he did know.

Moments later when he probably should have just let the topic slide, he said, "She wants me to give her away."

Layla shifted. "What about your dad?"

Sam dry-washed his face with his hands. "He has some tests or something that day. His health hasn't been the best lately and his doctor doesn't think it's a good idea if he flies."

"So why doesn't your sister reschedule the wedding?"

Why not, indeed? "Because she's stubborn. Probably thinks Mom and Dad are making the health problems up so she won't marry Dumbo."

"Ah."

"Yeah, ah."

Silence reigned as Sam mulled over the situation. He hadn't talked to Heather since the day at the pier, yet, as promised, she'd sent him a wedding invitation. No small note. No indication that they'd even had the conversation they'd had. Just a subtle, handmade notice that said she was tossing the ball into his court and it was up to him to decide what to do. Either way, she was going to marry Brian.

"Would you like some company?"

Sam peeked out from where his arm covered his eyes again.

Layla was staring at the ceiling, not him. She shrugged as if talking to herself. "I'm really not big on weddings myself, but if you think it would help, I could come. I'd like to meet your sister."

Sam thought about that. "Do you think you can talk her out of marrying the moron?"

He watched her smile, still completely unaware that he was looking at her. "I think that falls a little outside my area of expertise." She squinted. "But I could try to make you feel better about the situation."

She turned her head in his direction. "How long have you been watching me?"

"Long enough." He gestured vaguely with his hand. "And how could you make me feel better about the situation?"

Her saucy smile made all sorts of naughty thoughts spring to mind. "Oh, I don't know. But I'm sure I can come up with something."

Just thinking about the dreaded event with her in the picture made him feel better. "I'd like that. For you to come to the wedding next month, I mean."

"With or without the promised, um, help?"

"Oh, definitely with."

He chuckled and playfully swatted her bare behind. She laughed and moved so that she was lying next to him. He peeked out from his arm again. She was still bare from the waist down, the neat wedge of dark hair glistening with the evidence of their passion. But she'd put her camisole back on.

Strange, this Dr. Hollister. She was perfectly comfortable running around bare-assed, but made a point of covering her breasts. And what marvelous breasts they were, too. If anyone were capable of judging in that category, he was. Layla's breasts might be on the small side, but what they lacked in quantity they made up for in quality. They were high and pert, her nipples large and provocative, making him want to swallow them and her whole.

But obviously she didn't feel the same.

"You know, I could enlarge your breasts for you, no problem."

LAYLA lay still for a long moment, her brain trying but failing to register the words Sam had just said. One minute they were discussing his sister and her coming nuptials. The next he was telling her she needed a boob job.

Her breathing went from rapid to nonexistent in two seconds flat—the time it had taken him to utter those fateful words.

"No problem..." she repeated, feeling her blood pick up speed in her veins. Only this time it had nothing to do with passion or soft cries or phenomenal orgasms or the possibility of connecting with

him on a level that transcended this very bedroom.
No. The motivation behind her quickened pulse rate
was Sam's careless words.

"Yeah, you know, maybe up you to a C-cup,"
he said, and she wondered if he'd gone daft in the
head. Was he really so blind that he couldn't see the
way her face was burning? The hard frown beginning to etch around her mouth?

"I wouldn't go any bigger than that, really. The
balloon look wouldn't go well with your slender
frame."

"Balloon look..." she echoed, her words sounding dangerously far away.

"An hour's work, a month of healing, and you'd
be as good as new in no time."

She finally looked at him, but he still had his
blasted arm over his eyes. "Don't you mean better
than new?"

Suddenly she was no longer on the bed next to
him, she was striding across the room, looking for
her panties. There, next to the pile of his clothes.

"You going for sustenance? If so, I could really
use a bottle of water."

"No," Layla said slowly, following her panties
with a short, blue silk robe. She tied it off with jerky
movements. "What you really need is to have your
fucking head examined."

The arm finally came off the eyes and he blinked
at her, completely clueless. "Uh-oh. What did I say
now?"

Layla began pacing the room, forth and back, back and forth, gathering her own discarded clothes. She snatched her blouse from the back of the chair then turned to stare at him. "Are you really that dense? Please tell me you're not, because I haven't reached the boiling point yet, but that would probably send me careening right over the edge."

He propped himself up on his elbows and watched her move like a madwoman around the room.

"I..." she snatched up her panty hose "...can't..." she nearly ripped her skirt where it was caught under the leg of the bed "...believe you just said that."

"Said what? About getting your breasts done?"

She pointed at him, the blouse she held swinging back and forth. "Bingo." She pulled in a deep breath, looked at the clothes in her hands, then back at him. "And you wondered why I didn't want to show you my breasts in the light?" She stabbed the air with her finger again. "That's why." She shook her head, paced a couple of feet one way, then back the other way. "The first time I show you and you couldn't wait to recommend bigger ta-tas."

He hadn't budged an inch except his eyes, which moved as he watched her pace. "What's the big deal? People do it all the time, Lay. Hell, I do it all the time for people. You knew...know that."

"Yeah, but for some godforsaken reason, I kept choosing to forget that small fact."

She stared at the clothes in her hands again. "Where am I going? This is *my* place." She strode toward her closet, opened the door, then dropped the items in a laundry hamper. "Save the world, have your breasts enlarged," she muttered under her breath as she stuffed the stray foot of her hose into the basket then slammed the door shut.

She swung around to find Sam still watching her from the bed. "Are you still here?"

He blinked. "You wanted me to go?"

She gaped at him. "Well, yeah." She tapped a finger against her forehead. "You know, for a doctor, you're a little slow on the uptake. Do you know that, Lovejoy?"

She shivered, then cursed herself for doing so.

He slowly swung his legs over the side of the bed. "Shit," he said, as if to himself. "The nose."

Layla stared at him as if he'd just lost a few more marbles. "What?" She raised a hand. "Wait. If it has anything to do with fixing my nose, too, at a two-for-one discount or something, I have to warn you that you're putting your life in serious danger."

"No. I meant I'd forgotten your reaction that first night at the bar. You know, when I asked if your nose was the real thing. You nearly tossed your soda in my face."

"I wish I had."

He ran his hands through his hair a few times then rubbed the back of his neck. "I'm getting the feeling

I'm going to wish the same by the time this night's over.''

''Oh? What makes you think it isn't already?'' She opened a drawer, took out fresh lingerie, then slammed the drawer shut again. ''I'm going to take a shower. By the time I get out, I want you to be nothing but a distant memory.''

''Lay—''

''Ah. Not a word, Lovejoy. I don't want to hear a single word.''

''Can I call you later?''

She slammed the door to the bedroom for good measure as she left it, intending that to be her answer.

SURELY one throwaway comment wasn't enough to topple ten days' worth of relationship building.

The following afternoon Sam picked up his car keys and hurried out the front door of his house in the Hills. What was he talking about, relationship building? He and Layla had been having great sex. Nothing more, nothing less.

Only that instead of getting worse as it always had before, it kept getting better.

And last night when she'd kicked him out of her bed and her apartment, he'd felt like pure crap, unable to sleep a wink and he hadn't had a thing to eat since the previous day's lunch.

''The woman is a menace,'' he said, pushing the

remote to unlock the doors to his Jag, then climbing behind the wheel.

Hell, he didn't think she needed the breast enlargement. She'd been the one so self-conscious about her breasts that she'd hidden them from him whenever the light had been switched on. He started the car and turned up the volume of his Sting CD. While he normally didn't recommend the surgery to women who were shy of their bodies, he figured Layla, being the physician she was, was adult enough to know her own mind.

And, oh boy, had he ever been right there.

Unfortunately he hadn't spotted what that was until she was nearly pulling the sheets out from underneath him.

Despite her demand that he leave while she was showering, he'd gotten dressed and stuck around, getting himself a water and parking it on the sofa waiting for her to come out.

Only the long shower had done nothing to improve her mood. If anything, she was even more irate at finding him still there.

He'd merely held up his hands, grabbed his car keys, and left.

And, ever since, he'd wondered what he could have done differently.

He skillfully maneuvered the winding road that led to the Hollywood freeway, the windows down despite the warm air. Traffic was light even for a Sunday and he was thankful. He didn't think he'd be up for battling with L.A. traffic right about now. Hell, he wouldn't be up to much of anything until he cleared the air between him and Layla.

Of course, it would help if she'd picked up her phone the two times he'd called last night, and the three times he'd called this morning. Instead he'd been reduced to leaving messages on her machine, probably coming off sounding like an even bigger fool. And obviously having zero impact because she hadn't called him back.

Miles disappeared under the finely tuned, twelve-cylinder engine. Honestly, he didn't know why he had bothered. He would be seeing her in, he glanced at his watch, in ten minutes anyway.

He only hoped she wasn't holding a gun when he rounded the corner to her father's house in Beverly Hills.

13

DAMN, damn, damn.

Layla tugged at her beige linen skirt where it was caught in her car door. A tiny ripping sound made her cringe. After digging in her purse for her keys, she unlocked and opened the door, forcing the aging Pontiac to relinquish its hold.

Things had not been going well since she'd booted Sam out of her apartment last night. First, she'd paced the floor until all hours, finally earning an irritated knock and shout from her downstairs neighbor. Then, when she'd finally crawled into bed, she'd lain there staring at the ceiling replaying Sam's suggestion over and over again in her mind. She'd finally fallen into an exhausted sleep around five, only to dream about saline implants with tiny silver wings flying all around her. She'd batted at them and batted at them, and woken up to find herself soaked from the glass of water she'd knocked over on her bedside table.

Never, ever, had a man made her feel so...self-conscious about her appearance before. So, okay, yes, she'd been hesitant to bare her breasts to him when the lights were on. Strangely enough, she'd never felt that way with other guys she'd dated. It had never even been an issue. But being involved with the infamous boob doctor brought along its own set of luggage. And while, yes, even she thought her behavior was a little…odd, the small move to hold down her camisole the first time had snowballed into much much more until it had become an issue all its own.

It didn't help that her irrational fear had been verified and then some when Sam had made his unwelcome suggestion that she have her breasts enlarged.

She brushed at her narrow skirt then slammed her car door, finding some satisfaction in the action. She realized she'd done a lot of slamming since last night. Doors, drawers, it didn't matter, so long as it made noise and could handle the abuse. It was a far sight better than hitting Sam over the head with the stuffed Tweety Reilly had given her for Christmas one year. Or impaling him with the vibrator Mallory had given her for her last birthday. Or blindsiding him with the baseball bat Jack had brought over after a neighbor had been burglarized.

Men.

Okay, so she couldn't cram them all onto the same sinking boat. But for a lot of men, it was all about the package. Forget about what was inside. As long as a woman had a great pair of bazoombas, all was right with the world.

She heard a low growling sound. She looked

around her father's mammoth Beverly Hills estate, from the curving driveway that held a limo and a Bentley, to the Italian marble fountain just beyond that, to the neat shrubs lining the three-story stone structure designed to look like an Irish castle. Her father, the king of medical research. All he needed was a moat and a crown and he'd be all set. Oh, wait, he already had the crown. A jewel-encrusted replica of Henry VIII's that her stepmother Sharon had bought for him.

How apropos.

She grimaced as the growling sound got louder. Had her father bought a couple of dogs to round out the picture? No, she realized with a start, the growling was coming from her.

Well, that was pretty, wasn't it? Overnight she'd turned into a snarling shrew.

She cleared her throat, pulled in a deep breath of the warm October air and did a yoga stretch for her neck. One hour and she'd be out of there. One hour and…

The sound of a car driving up caught her attention. As it pulled to a stop behind hers and the engine was shut off, she realized she was growling again.

Sam was here.

BOY, he couldn't have timed his arrival better, Sam thought as he climbed out of his Jag. Two minutes earlier and Layla would have still been in her car and probably would have run over him if the murderous expression on her beautiful face was anything to go by.

As she advanced on him at full throttle, he didn't know if her being without a car would make a difference.

"What are you doing here?" she asked, her color high, her sinfully lovely green eyes flashing.

Sam cocked a brow, wondering how much he should worry about physical injury. "I'm here for the same reason you are. Or have you forgotten?"

She shifted her weight from one foot to the other. "What is it with people questioning my memory capacities lately?" She leveled a stare at him. "Of course, I know the reason you're here. But if you had one ounce of decency in that…in that… handsome body of yours, you'd have called and cancelled first thing this morning."

Handsome body? Sam cocked a grin. "Maybe if someone else I was trying to reach had answered my calls I would have thought about canceling."

"So you're putting this on me?"

"No. I'm just saying the thought hadn't occurred to me because I was otherwise occupied."

"Sam!"

The booming voice from the open doorway of the house captured both their attentions. Layla's father walked down the two stone steps and made his way out to greet them.

"So glad you could make it, son," the older man said, pumping his hand.

"Actually," Layla said as she kissed her father's cheek when he turned to her, "Sam was just coming by to say that something's come up—last-minute, you know—and he won't be staying for dinner after all."

"Not staying? Rubbish! Whatever it is can wait until he has some fine food in his stomach."

Sam eyed Layla, weighing his options. Stay here and piss her off further. Or go and leave her as pissed as she was before. Difficult call. If he left, he might not have an opportunity to make things right with her, considering she had a thing for not returning calls. If he stayed, he might end up filleted and eaten alive.

Thomas made his decision for him as he heartily patted him on the back. "Come on inside. Sharon's due to come downstairs any moment. And she does so like to make an entrance."

Sam caught the rolling of Layla's eyes. It seemed he wasn't the only one she felt animosity for. Equally distributed animosity was good.

She caught him looking at her and he grinned.

He swore he could feel the burn of her glare against his skin.

"You didn't have trouble finding the place, I trust?" Thomas asked, completely ignorant of the hostile vibes emanating from his daughter. Either that or he was used to ignoring them.

"No, no. Not at all. Just a hop, skip and a jump away, really."

"Good." Thomas motioned for Layla to precede him and Sam followed.

No matter how many mansions Sam stepped inside, he always felt momentarily awestruck. The three-bedroom, hundred-year-old house in the working-class section of Toledo, Ohio, where he'd grown up had done nothing to prepare him for the grandiose status of doctors' houses in L.A. and the surrounding areas. Each one was more opulent than the last.

He slid his right hand casually into his pocket. Of course, if he often felt as if he'd stepped into the sterile environment of a hotel, he wasn't about to admit it to his host.

He glanced at Layla to find her looking uncomfortable.

Hmm... Revealing, that.

"Sharon, darling? Our guests have arrived."

Sam felt as though he was caught in a time-warp episode of *Dynasty* and Thomas was Blake Carrington, his wife, Krystle. Only, the woman who appeared at the top of the winding staircase looked more like Joan Collins. He hadn't spoken to her much when they'd crossed paths at social gatherings, so he really couldn't say if she was more like Krystle or Alexis in temperament. Although, given the staging of her grand entrance, he was afraid she might be Alexis.

He rubbed his chin, wondering who wore a ten-thousand-dollar suit to a simple Sunday dinner. He suppressed the urge to thwack his forehead. Oh, wait a minute. He'd forgotten. He was in L.A.

He grimaced at the uncharacteristic sarcasm. His thoughts were more in line with what he could imagine Layla thinking or saying. He squinted at her as Alexis, er, Sharon made her way down the two-story red-carpet-covered marble stairs, wondering if she was starting to rub off on him.

But, amazingly enough, she looked far more relaxed than she had moments before.

Hmm…

Midway through dinner in the gigantic dining room at a table that could easily seat thirty, Sam found himself thinking *hmm* to himself a lot. Layla aside, Thomas and Sharon had no children, and the patronizing way they treated Layla made even Sam uncomfortable. But Layla herself appeared more than used to it as she kept her gaze on the never-ending courses of food that were served and listened to her stepmother drone on about her charitable endeavors.

Sam cleared his throat. "Layla was just telling me that one of the staff physicians at the clinic has left."

Dead silence fell on the table as Layla gaped at him, and Thomas and Sharon's mouths snapped shut.

Thomas dabbed at the corners of his mouth with

a napkin. "Are you still working at that clinic, Elizabeth? I thought you'd planned to stop last year."

Uh-oh.

"I'm still putting some hours in there," Layla responded to her father, although her gaze was on Sam.

But rather than the hostility he would have expected, she seemed genuinely puzzled.

He gave a small shrug. He honestly couldn't say why he'd said what he had. It's just that since they'd gotten there, he hadn't heard one genuine question asked of Layla about her personal or professional life. Rather, Sharon rattled on, asking if she could practice her newly acquired French skills on them, not even acknowledging that Layla easily conversed with her in the foreign language, and politely corrected her every now and again. Then Thomas had gone on to talk about what was going on at the country club. And with each word and every laugh, Sam had begun to itch. Had even caught himself scratching his arm through his long-sleeved shirt.

"How sweet," Sharon cooed, finally responding to the news that Layla still worked at the clinic.

Sweet? Sam looked at the woman. Definitely Alexis.

But why would Layla look more relaxed after her stepmother had joined them? He'd figured she must share a closer relationship with her stepmother than with her father. But given what he'd seen over the past hour, that definitely wasn't the case.

He suppressed himself from making a face. His parents had raised him not to judge others. But as he sat there with Layla, he had an odd sense that she had somehow climbed inside his head and was coloring his thoughts in a way no one had before.

He looked at his watch. "Oh, look at the time," he said with a long sigh. "You know, Thomas, I hate to say it, but Layla…Elizabeth was right about something coming up. I really hate to ruin this marvelous dinner, but I'm afraid I'm going to have to run."

Sharon blinked. "But there are two more courses yet to serve."

Across from him Layla sighed softly. He wiped his mouth then put his napkin on the table.

"I apologize for having to take your daughter away, as well. I'm sure the three of you don't have much time for socializing, what with your busy schedules, but I really need her help in this matter."

"What matter?" Thomas asked.

Layla's smile of relief was so all-encompassing, Sam felt his heartbeat kick up a notch. "Now, is that any question to ask of a guest, Father?"

She got up from the table and kissed first her stepmother on the cheek, then her father. "We're really sorry. I'll call sometime this week."

Sam led the way out. The moment the door closed behind them, Layla threw her arms around him and gave him a big, wet, loud kiss.

Startled, it took him a minute to regain his bearings. "What was that for?"

"For saving my life."

He grinned down at her and began to put his hands on her hips to draw her closer. "Well, if I'd known I'd get a response like that, I would have done this five minutes into the cucumber soup."

She stepped out of his reach. "Come on," she said.

He raised his brows. Looked like things were going to get a whole lot better, fast.

"I want you to follow me to my place, then we'll take my car from there."

No sex. Damn.

He rubbed his chin with his index finger. Of course, she could be wanting to have sex in a strange and exotic place.

That put the smile back on his face as he climbed into his Jag and followed her down the curving drive and out the huge iron gates.

"DEFINITELY NOT an exotic place. Strange, maybe. But not exotic."

Layla drifted her old Pontiac to a stop in the fifty-year-old trailer park in North Hollywood. Across the lane sat a brown-and-white mobile home that looked like it hadn't been mobile for decades.

"Pardon me?" she said, looking at Sam.

He was looking around at the car-sized potholes in the narrow roads, the overgrown grass and weeds in between most of the homes, the beat-up cars that lined the lane. Ten or so lots up was, as the owner-slash-manager referred to it, a park. Essentially it consisted of two empty lots holding an old tire swing that hung from a rusty bar and a wood bench that bore two decades' worth of carved initials.

"Considering a change of residence?" Sam asked. He watched three teenage girls wearing tight cutoff jeans, tight halter tops and overdone makeup as they passed the car, openly considering the passengers. Layla had little doubt that had Sam been alone, they would have approached the car and talked to him.

"Actually, I brought you here to even out the impression you must have gotten at my father's."

He slowly moved his gaze back to her face. "Can I ask you a question first?"

"Sure."

"Why did you relax when Sharon joined us?"

She blinked at him. "What?"

"You were all…I don't know, prickly when you greeted your dad in the driveway—actually, you were prickly with him the other day at the office as well—but when your stepmother came down the stairs you relaxed."

It took her a minute to switch gears. To move from what she'd been about to say to answer his odd question. Finally, she shrugged and said, "I don't know. I've never really given it much thought before." Is that what she'd done? "Maybe one-on-

one with my father I never feel like I measure up. But when Sharon joins us, my father's distracted and…''

''And you can just step back and lay low.''

Now that was a way of putting things. ''I think that observation hits a little too close to home.''

Sam turned to look out the window. She followed his gaze to where another teen girl had joined the three along with a toddler.

''I used to be one of those girls,'' she said quietly.

She felt Sam's surprised gaze on her profile, but she didn't acknowledge him. ''That trailer there?'' She nodded toward the one across the lane. ''My mother still lives there. This place, this park…this is where I did most of my growing up.''

She thought she heard Sam murmur a curse word, but she couldn't be sure.

''When things started, well, going well for me, I tried to move Trudy in with me, you know? But she wouldn't hear of it.'' She gave a weak smile. ''Said you can take the girl out of the trailer park, but you can't take the trailer park out of the girl. So she was staying right where she was, thank you very much.''

''Independent woman, your mother.''

''Stubborn woman, my mother.''

''Explains a lot.''

Layla looked at him, surprised to find herself smiling instead of angry. ''That trait could come just as easily from my father, you know.''

"Unfortunately dinner today also revealed a lot."
He gestured toward the trailer. "Are we going in?"

"Um, no. Trudy's not home. She's at work. At a
bar."

Layla sat for a long moment, feeling as though
she'd left the trailer park just yesterday, yet also
finding it hard to believe she'd ever lived there at
all. Finally, she shifted in her seat to face Sam.

"See those girls in the park?"

Sam tossed another glance at them.

"Well, maybe what I'm about to say will help
you understand a little more about me. Where I
come from. Why I have the opinions I do."

Sam held up his hand. "You don't need to explain yourself to me, Layla."

"No, you're right. I don't. But I...I don't know,
I want to tell you anyway." She quietly cleared her
throat. "You see, growing up here, with parents who
work all the time making no better than minimum
wage, and who, when they're not working, are too
exhausted to really contribute to their children's up-
bringing, and who are mostly divorced. Or in the
case of my mom, were never married... Well, it all
combines to make for a vicious cycle and a unique
environment."

She paused and absently rubbed a spot on the
steering wheel with her thumb.

"I guess what I'm trying to say is that those girls
are probably no older than fourteen or fifteen at
most—"

"No way."

She cracked a sad smile. "Way. If they were older, they'd be on welfare or working nickel-and-dime jobs themselves." She allowed her words to sink in. "You see, when you're that age, with nothing but your peers and the television and movies as your guides, well, the only way you see out—and they all want out—is either to sleep or marry your way out."

He narrowed his eyes at her. "I don't understand."

She pointed to the girl on the end. "See the one with the baby? I had a friend, Tricia, who got pregnant at age thirteen. The father was eighteen and she was convinced that if she had his baby, he'd marry her, they'd move to his trailer and the three of them would live happily ever after."

"Let me guess. It didn't happen that way."

She shook her head. "No. He basically denied paternity, she ended up hooking to make ends meet, got into drugs, ultimately had her little girl taken away and within a blink of an eye became another sad statistic when she overdosed a year later after a john beat her up."

She sat for a long moment, her eyes burning, her throat thick. That series of events had taken place years ago, and she'd been in college when she'd found out about Tricia's suicide. But none of that made it any less intense. She looked out the side window away from Sam until she could breathe again without hurting. Then she turned back to him. "To these girls? The only thing about themselves that they think is worth anything is their bodies. They see their parents working dead-end jobs for barely enough cash to squeak by and think that road's not for them. And," she said with great emphasis, "if you offered them a free boob job, they'd be clawing over each other to get it."

She took a deep breath.

"They're the ones who strip in the clubs down the street. The ones you see hoping to get their big chance by becoming groupies. In videos, shaking everything they got as hard as they can, praying that it's better than the other girls'.

"And they were me."

She stared through the windshield at the four teenagers, feeling such an ache in her chest that she was afraid it might collapse in on itself. She sensed Sam's gaze on her, but couldn't bring herself to look at him.

"Then your father stepped in."

She finally looked toward him, but focused on a spot on his shirt rather than gaze into his eyes. "No. That's when my mother dumped me on my father's doorstep, and he had no choice but to step in. If she hadn't done that...if he hadn't taken me in..." She took a deep, steadying breath and waved her hand. "You get the picture."

"We might never have met."

"We for sure would never have met." She

cleared her throat and curved her fingers around the steering wheel, thinking of herself now, and of herself then. She remembered why her mom had dumped her on her father. She'd stopped wearing her glasses and had shed the studious look, gotten her hair cut like the singer Madonna's and worn Madonna clothes and makeup. And she'd slept with nearly every boy in the trailer park before she was fifteen. She'd known it all. She'd known nothing.

And now? Well, now she knew only one thing for certain. That she couldn't see Sam again.

"And it's for that reason, for everything I've told you, for what you've seen today that I... What exists between us must end."

14

SAM stared at Layla, trying to follow the dots she'd laid out in a neat little line, but getting lost in the vast whiteness between them.

"What?" he asked after he'd sat stupefied for what seemed like an eternity.

She tucked her chin into her chest. "I said, that's the reason—"

"I didn't mean I wanted you to repeat it. The first time was enough," he said, running his hands restlessly through his hair. He slid her a wary glance. "You're serious, aren't you?"

Her green eyes held sadness and resolution. "One hundred percent."

"And the reason is your upbringing..." he prompted, grasping at straws.

"The reason is that we're two completely different people. You see the world one way. I see it another." He heard her swallow. "Oh, we seem perfectly capable of putting all that aside when we're in bed, but..." She trailed off. "But that isn't enough, is it?"

Sam allowed another eon to pass as he digested everything she'd said. Birds sang, laughter sounded in the distance, and the interior of the car was so silent he might have been alone. And with each tick of his watch his own anger began to rise. Layla might have been the one upset last night and early today, but it was his turn. In fact, it was long past his turn.

He made a sound between a humorless laugh and a snort.

"What?" Layla asked.

Sam shook his head. "You know, for someone who has been through so much in your life, you still really don't have a clue, do you?"

She blinked at him, clearly shocked. "I—"

He held up a hand. "No. You've had your say. Now it's time I had mine."

He rested his hand on the seat back, near enough to touch her but not touching her. Touching her was the last thing on his mind just then. A first for him.

"You have it all figured out, don't you, Layla? You grew up here, but were also raised for a short time not only on the other side of the tracks, but way on the other side. You were given a priceless insight that you could use for good, but instead you use it to hide behind."

"That's hitting below the belt."

"Is it? I don't think so. I think it's hitting right where you need to be hit."

She reached out to start the car but he stayed her with a quick hand on her arm.

"Hear me out before you go fuming off into another one of your fits."

Probably not the wisest thing to say, but, damn it, he was pissed.

"First of all, I want to get something straight here. Last night when I...when I suggested what I did, I didn't do it because I wanted to see your breasts bigger. No. I thought you were unhappy with the size of your breasts and offered it up as an option. Nothing more; nothing less." He jabbed his thumb into his chest. "Unlike you, I happen to like your damn ta-tas just the way they are, thank you very much." He tried to calm himself. "But that's beside the point, isn't it?" he muttered.

She blinked at him, appearing to be trying to absorb what he was saying. By her expression, she seemed caught between wariness and a need to believe.

"Where was I?" he muttered to himself, hating that he'd veered so far off track. "Oh, yes. Insights..."

He struggled to collect his thoughts. Somewhere in the back of his mind he knew this was his one shot. Not only to make his point, but also to make it in a way that would either bring her back into his life for good, or chase her away from him forever.

"Do you color your hair?"

She blinked at him, her fingers touching the dark strands. "I've had it highlighted once or twice."

"Do you wear makeup?"

"Of course, but I..."

"Have you ever bought one of those damn push-up bras?"

Her mouth slapped closed.

"You know, on the surface you come off as easy-going. Live and let live and all that. But when you dig a little deeper, you get to truth, don't you? This isn't about those teenaged girls out there and their seemingly limited options, is it? And it's not about the superficiality of plastic surgery, big breasts, tucks and face-lifts either. This is about your need to place the blame on somebody for what you see as the shortcomings of your own life, your own up-bringing. You can't blame your mother because you love her, and in your mind she's untouchable. You can't blame your father because he was prevented from seeing you when you were young, and when he was asked to step up to the plate, he did, no matter that you don't approve of the way he did it."

An older woman towing a portable shopping cart behind her passed by his window and he paused, glancing at her but not really seeing her. Not really seeing anything but the words streaming through his head.

"Sam, I—"

"I'm not near done," he said quietly. He blew out a long breath. "Oh, you essentially work two full-time jobs—that's how much you put into that free clinic. And, yes, while that's generous and good-hearted of you, it also allows you to read through those rag magazines and smirk at the garbage in them, because, well, you're a good person deep down, aren't you, because you volunteer at a free clinic? And what's the matter with being a little snarky now and again?" He looked at her. "The problem is, I'm beginning to think snarky is your middle name."

Layla blinked several times as if unable to come up with a response. Finally, she said, "Define 'snarky.'"

"Cynical. Bitter. Judgmental."

She gasped and it was clear by the high color in her cheeks that she was quickly reaching his level of irritation.

"Tell me something, Layla. If I had told you who I was straight off the bat at that bar that night, would you have even given me a second glance? Or would you have smacked a label on me that said Unacceptable and never given me a second glance?"

Her eyes narrowed, but she didn't respond.

"Now, let me tell you something. I'm proud of what I've accomplished in my life to date, including all the surgery I've performed, corrective or cosmetic. Over the years people have come to me, unhappy with themselves and their lives and hoping that I could make it better for them. And I was happy to be able to help them. Maybe it's not what you would do. Hell, it's never something you would do. But it was their decision. Not yours. Not mine."

She jerkily crossed her arms over her chest, her eyes suspiciously bright.

She was a blink away from crying, he realized, and he felt the ice storm swirling within him begin to dissipate.

But he couldn't stop now. No. Stopping now would accomplish nothing.

He reached out and hooked a finger under her chin, forcing her to look at him.

"I'm going to ask you a question, Layla, and I want you to answer me honestly," he said softly.

He watched the battle for control behind her eyes.

"Did you ever expect us to last beyond a few dates?"

She made a small sniffling sound, then her chin came up. "No."

All the anger drained from Sam's muscles and he slumped briefly against the seat back.

"Well, then, that says it all, doesn't it? Because once you, Layla Hollister, believe anything, it's as good as the God-given truth. And nothing I could ever have done would have stopped the end from coming."

He reached for the car-door handle and opened it, stopping briefly to look at her.

"You know, I've never been here before either, on this strange emotional plane. I had no idea when we started dating that I would end up feeling the way I do about you. But at least I didn't fight it every step of the way. If anything, I tried to prolong it. Tried to help it develop into something even more powerful.''

She looked away and he didn't try to stop her.

''Yes, that means I'm saying I love you, Layla. I never knew what that meant before now, before you, but those fluff love experts are right in that it's not something you can define, you just know. And I do know that much is true.''

Her expression of surprise was nearly his undoing. He tightened his fingers on the door handle.

''But you...but you latched on to any excuse you could to stop this thing between us in its tracks. And I'm convinced that if it hadn't been my innocent remark last night, something else would have popped up. Something you could grab hold of and use to chase me away.''

He felt a sadness so complete sweep over him, it hurt his heart just to beat.

''I don't know. Maybe it's because you're afraid. Maybe it's that you can't trust something so indefinable yet with the power to hurt you so deeply. But you were right about one thing—there is no tomorrow for us.''

He climbed from the car and quietly closed the door.

LAYLA SAT pole-straight in the car, feeling the afternoon heat press in on her from all sides. Her throat felt so tight she could barely draw air into her lungs as she watched Sam walk away, moving along the same lane she had so many times growing up. His steps were long, his shoulders squared. The four teenage girls popped to attention as he neared and he greeted them before moving on farther.

Go get him, a tiny voice ordered her.

"I can't," she whispered to the empty air.

Early in their conversation, she'd accused Sam of hitting below the belt. It seemed strange that that's the way she felt. Only the blow had landed squarely on her solar plexus, robbing her of air, paralyzing her. She'd been prepared to watch him walk away. Her entire intention in bringing him to where she had grown up had been to end things. But she'd never planned on the utter and complete pain that pulsed in her chest.

She absently heard a car pull up behind hers and a door slam, but she couldn't tear her gaze away from Sam as he rounded a corner and moved out of sight.

"Layla?" a familiar female voice asked. "Is that you?"

She tried to pry her hands from the steering wheel as she looked through the open passenger window. "Oh, Mama, what have I done?"

TRUDY PUT an old, cracked Planter's Peanuts mug of tea down in front of Layla then took the chair across from her. "You know, I never did understand why you push yourself so hard."

An hour and two cups of caffeine-free tea had

passed since Sam had said what he had and walked away from her without looking back. She glanced around the old trailer for the first time since her mother had ushered her in. Everything looked old and worn and the same as it always had. Only now it also looked cozy, familiar…like home.

She and her mother sat in the dining room/kitchen at the front of the trailer with its country-style and careworn table and chairs. And though Layla couldn't see it, she knew that if she walked through the doorway to her left, she'd be in the living room with its brown carpeting and plain beige furniture. Pictures of her from kindergarten to college graduation would be all over the place in the same frames they'd always been in. And if she crossed to the back hallway, she'd find what had been her room, still with the same wood paneling, twin bed and posters of teen idols taped to the walls. Farther down was the bathroom and at the back was her mother's room.

And despite that the place was only a trailer and so unlike her father's lavish mansion, this would always be home to her. She pushed her bangs away from her face. Somewhere down the line she'd forgotten that. Forgotten the Christmases with her mother putting together the silver artificial tree because she didn't believe in killing anything for a few weeks' pleasure. Had let slip from her mind the echoes of laughter, of her doing her homework at the same table she sat at now, of her mother bathing her in the tub when she was little. Over the years she'd come only to think of her difficult teenage years, and had felt trapped and helpless and hopeless. And ultimately betrayed by a mother who had only been trying to do what was best for her by sending her to her father's.

And it *had* turned out to be best.

Only she had never really acknowledged that, had she? Had never taken a close look at it all and seen it as it really was.

How long had it been since she'd actually visited her mother? Oh, sure, she met her for breakfast or lunch or even dinner, but usually at restaurants located in between the trailer and her apartment, the rationale being that it was too far a drive for them either way. And she had been so busy...

So busy running from the past that she'd never stopped to realize that there was no longer anything to run from.

So busy making herself a professional success that her emotional development had remained as stunted as the fifteen-year-old she'd once been. The vulnerable, clean-scrubbed naive fifteen-year-old who'd stood on her father's doorstep clutching that small suitcase that had held all of her belongings. At least that's how she had seen it. The truth was that her belongings could never be packed in a case of any size. Her belongings remained with both her mother and father and, yes, she realized with a spark of pain, Sam.

"Maybe it's because you never thought I did enough," her mother broke the silence.

Layla blinked at her. Time had taken its toll on Trudy Thompson. Her hair was graying, wrinkles were deepening. But no passage of time could ever take away the warmth in her eyes and the happiness in her smile. Even if that smile now held a tinge of sadness.

"What did you say?" she asked.

Her mother took a sip of her own tea. "I said that maybe the reason you always pushed yourself so hard was because you felt I wasn't doing enough."

"Oh, God, never!" She reached out for her mother's hand, realizing in that one moment that they had never really touched much. Not casually. Not the way she and Mallory, Reilly and Jack did.

She tightened her grip, determined that from now on that was going to change.

"I always knew you were doing the best you could," she said.

Trudy turned her hand over so she could return Layla's grasp, as if considering the new demonstration and deciding she liked it, as well. "No, I didn't, Layla." She looked up at her. "Not the way you would have liked me to. I always knew you wished I would go back to school, move out of this trailer, to somehow…what was the word you used once? Oh, yes. *Better* myself." She squeezed her hand. "But what you never understood was that I was— and am—happy right where I am. I like tending bar.

Or working at a Laundromat. Or waitressing. I like this trailer and the memories it holds.'' She gazed at her. ''And I think that's something you really never got. You always wanted more.'' She laughed. ''And you got it.''

Had she? And if she had, at what price?

They sat there for a long while, neighborhood cars coming and going, the old orange-and-rhinestone cat clock whose tail no longer moved ticking off the time on the wall, their hands intertwined.

THE FOLLOWING MORNING Layla blinked as a bright shaft of light cut across her pillow. She held a hand up against it then realized what the light meant and scrambled out of bed, the top sheet wound around her legs, nearly bringing her straight down.

''Oh, God,'' she muttered, squinting at the clock. Ten. Not nine-thirty, or nine-forty-five, but ten. And she was two hours late for work at the Center.

She disentangled herself from the sheets with a loud tear of fabric then rushed one way and the next, gathering her clothes, her shoes, then dumping them outside the bathroom door. Before she stripped out of her nightshirt she eyed the answering machine. One message.

Her heart skipped a beat. She hugged herself with her arms. Did she dare listen to it? Was it Sam telling her they needed to talk? And what would she do if it was him?

Yesterday, when he'd walked away from her, felt

like an eon ago instead of just a few, tortured hours. She'd stayed with Trudy at the trailer late into the night, allowing her mom to feed her fried chicken, mashed potatoes and corn, and tons of sympathy. She'd come home half expecting to find Sam waiting for her, or at least a message on her machine. Nothing.

And now as the numeral 1 steadily burned, she was afraid it was him.

So much to absorb. So much to *do*.

Remembering the time, she left the message where it was and ran for the shower, just getting her nightshirt and panties off before stepping under the punishing, cool spray. It always took so long for the hot water to come through. And when it did, she usually had to hurry to adjust the water so she wouldn't scald herself.

Had anyone ever talked to her the way Sam had yesterday? Said the things he had? Reilly? Mallory? Jack? No. Everyone seemed content to accept her the way she was. Then again, she hadn't slept with any of them. Sam had a unique perspective when it came to her. But still, was two weeks enough time for someone to get to know anyone else?

She quickly rinsed and yanked open the curtain. Cop-out. Major cop-out, as Mallory would say. While she could spend the next two lifetimes arguing the details, one fact rang completely and utterly true: Sam had not only come to know her well, he had come to know her too well.

And he loved her.

Layla shivered as she dried off. She caught her sluggish moves and ordered her muscles to quicken the pace.

The man had never before been the first to say, "I love you." As was the case in the majority of male-female relationships, she'd always been the one to profess her love first. Then the man usually ran full-out in the other direction. This scenario had played out three times in her life.

But Sam...

Not only had Sam not hesitated to say the words, she'd had no doubts whatsoever that he'd meant them. He hadn't been trying to sleep with her. Or trying to talk her into doing something she wasn't inclined to do. He had looked at her point-blank and told her he loved her.

And then he'd told her goodbye.

The telephone rang in the other room. Layla's throat tightened, imagining Sam on the other end, waiting for her to answer. How long had it been ringing? Had she been so out of it that she hadn't heard it? Or had the shower muffled the sound?

She stepped into a pair of panties, grabbed her camisole, then padded out to pick up the receiver.

"Hello?" she answered before she could rationalize herself out of it.

She was greeted be the tinny sound of the dial tone. She slowly replaced the receiver and watched the answering machine number. It didn't budge from one.

"Listen to it already," she whispered.

She punched the button then hugged herself as if for protection from whatever might be waiting for her.

"Dr. Hollister? This is Traci from the Center. Is everything all right?" A pause, then, "I'm transferring your morning patients to the other physicians, but if you could please give me a call as soon as you get this...."

Her assistant. Not Sam.

Layla picked up the phone to call Traci, eyeing the stack of mail on the table next to the answering machine. An unopened bank statement lay on top. She absently picked it up as she dialed the number.

"Trident Medical Center."

"Traci? Hi, it's Layla."

"Dr. Hollister! I've been worried sick. I mean, you're never late and I wasn't sure what to do. For all I knew you could be lying on the floor dying or something—"

Layla smiled vaguely at Traci's rush of words. "It's all right. I'm okay." She ran her fingers through her damp hair then opened the end of the bank statement with her thumbnail. "I just overslept, that's all."

"Overslept?" the assistant said, as if the word were completely foreign to her.

Actually, up until fifteen minutes ago, Layla herself hadn't been all that familiar with the word. Not once in her life had she ever overslept.

She slid the statement out of the envelope then shook the folded page to straighten it out.

"So I should expect you soon, then?" Traci asked.

"Mmm," Layla responded distractedly, following the column of lines down to the bottom one. Her eyes widened and she made a strangled sound.

"Dr. Hollister?"

The statement drifted from her fingers to land on the floor. There was no way... It was impossible that...

Oh, God...

"Dr. Hollister, are you still there?"

"Traci? Actually, I won't be in this morning," she said, her voice barely above a whisper. "In fact, I'm going to take the day off. Suddenly, you know, I'm not feeling too well."

"Oh. Okay."

It took two tries for Layla to hang up the phone, then she slid down the wall to sit on the floor, the statement seeming to wink at her in the bright morning light.

It seemed that while she wasn't looking, the few dollars she'd tucked away had procreated and multiplied into quite a few other dollars.

Suddenly, Layla needed to do some serious thinking. Sam's words yesterday had started her wondering about some of the choices she'd made. Now this money—this incredible amount of money—had just given her the resources to make some significant changes. Yes, she needed to do some thinking.

Right now.

Well, just as soon as she could gather enough strength to scrape herself off the floor....

15

SAM LOOKED at his watch, then at Layla's closed office door, his frown so deep it hurt his face. He hadn't gotten any sleep at all the night before, and he felt it. And the fact that his little ruse to run into the frustrating Dr. Hollister accidentally was about to fail miserably only made matters worse.

He passed the receptionist's desk, then stopped, sighed, and backtracked again. "Is Dr. Hollister not in this morning?"

The pretty young brunette blinked. "She's out sick today, Dr. Lovejoy." She scrambled around on top of her desk. "Shall I take a message for her?"

Out sick? He ran his hand over his stubble-dotted chin. Being privy to all the staff's records, he knew that Layla had never missed a day in her five years at the Center.

"Nothing serious, I hope?" he asked.

The receptionist smiled. "I really couldn't say."

"I see. Okay," he said, sliding his hands into his pockets. "No, no message."

"Oh, boy, are you ever in it bad," his fellow physician Bill Gauge said as he pounded him on the back. Bill was the reason Sam had come up with to visit Layla's floor.

Sam blinked as he turned to face the other man. "What?" he fairly croaked.

"The office pool on who Nurse Betty will set her sights on next. I see you changed your bet again this morning."

Sam instantly relaxed. For a minute there he'd thought Bill was talking about... He pushed the thought from his mind. He couldn't think about what the staff might be saying about him and the pretty Dr. Layla Hollister on top of everything else going on just then.

"So what did you want to see me about?" Bill asked as they walked down the hall.

Sam mentally scrambled to get a grip. It hadn't been Bill he'd wanted to see at all, but Layla. And since he hadn't been able to do that...well, there was suddenly no reason to be there.

He patted Bill on the back and said, "Actually, I'm going to have to get back to you on that. Just got buzzed by Nancy and a staff meeting was pushed up."

"Oh, okay."

The only problem was, Sam felt that nothing was going to be okay again.

LATER that afternoon, Sam sat in his office staring at the dead plant on the corner of his desk. It was time to face facts. That plant was not going to miraculously come back to life and look as good as it had on the day Heather had given it to him without some serious attention. And neither was his fractured relationship with Heather.

As for Layla…

Well, he'd just up and beat the hell out of that one, hadn't he?

He winced and rubbed the pads of his index finger and thumb against his closed eyelids.

In the hours immediately after the incident, he'd felt pretty damn pleased with himself. He'd said what he'd wanted to say, and she hadn't stopped him from saying it. But then reality had begun to settle in somewhere around midnight as he lay in his bed—alone—and he realized that it didn't matter how right he'd been. He missed her.

A low groan exited his mouth as he leaned back in his chair.

Just where did he get off lecturing her? Lord knew his own life or past relationships weren't model material. But, damn it, when she'd told him they didn't have a future, something had snapped.

And a pain so acute, so burning, had burrowed so deeply inside him that he'd done the only thing he could just then: he'd lashed out.

"No time for a nap now," Nancy said, whisking into his office.

Sam popped an eye open, wondering if it was just him or if the papers on his desk stirred in the wind

Nancy created with her ceaseless movements. "I'm not napping."

"Excuse me. When one has one's eyes closed, it usually means one is asleep."

"I'm thinking."

"About whether to throw that plant away?"

He squinted at the dead leaves, wondering if he should finally admit that he'd killed the thing.

That he'd pretty much killed everything that had been good in his life.

"Here," she said, handing him a fax. "This just came in."

He saw the San Rafael Free Clinic's logo at the top and nearly catapulted himself over his desk as he sprang forward from his prone position.

It was from Layla.

"Can she do that?" Nancy asked, coming to stand over his left shoulder.

Sam blinked. "Can she do what?"

"Just quit like that."

He forced himself to concentrate on the words on the sheet. *Resignation* leapt at him and lodged in his throat.

"I mean, she's under contract with the Center, isn't she?"

Sam's headache doubled in size with each word Nancy said. "Can you get me some aspirin, Nancy?" he asked.

"Aspirin? Sure." She nudged him out of the way,

opened his lap drawer, then slapped a packet of two painkillers on the desk in front of him.

"Hmm."

Sam squinted up at her. "What?"

She shrugged, picked up the files in his out-box, fingered through them, put a sheet down and told him to sign, then said, "Just that if I needed verification before, I don't need it anymore."

Sam scrawled his name where she indicated, thinking he should probably start reading the stuff he signed. "What are you talking about?" he muttered.

She peeled the sheet off his blotter. "Oh, nothing. Just the rumors that are going around about you and the young, pretty Dr. Hollister."

"Hey, I'm young."

"Yes, but don't try to tell me you're pretty, no matter how attractive the female population thinks you are."

"What rumors about Layla and me?"

She smiled as she headed for the door. "A lady never gossips about such things. But if it helps any, my money's on you."

Money…

Sam watched the office door close behind Nancy then slumped back down in his chair, wondering if things could get any worse.

The telephone extension to his right rang and he snatched it up.

"Sam? It's Heather."

His sister. The one screwing up her life by marrying a moron. The one who wanted him to give her away at the wedding.

He tore open the aspirin packet with his teeth, thinking that yes, indeed, things could get much worse.

IT WAS Tuesday morning and Layla didn't have to be anywhere but right where she was. Which was in Sugar 'n' Spice waiting for Reilly to bring over coffee and sticky buns.

She tried for a smile. By all rights she should be thrilled right now. The sixteen-hour days she'd been putting in nonstop for the past three years were officially at an end. The only place she had to be was at the clinic, and that wasn't until three o'clock this afternoon. Which meant she could do anything she wanted, go anywhere she wanted, without worrying that she should be somewhere else.

She swallowed hard, wishing that something she wanted to do and someplace that she wanted to be wasn't connected to Dr. Sam Lovejoy in any way.

She shivered.

"So explain this to me again," Reilly said, seeming to have taken a long time to join her as she slid a wooden tray onto the bar-style table. "You don't work at the Center now because…"

Layla smiled as she took her coffee in both hands and deeply inhaled the sweet aroma. "Because I quit."

"You...quit," Reilly repeated, taking the seat opposite her. "Just like that. No warning. No real reason. You just up and left."

"Mmm-hmm." Layla blew on her coffee then took a sip of the hot liquid. "Very freeing. I highly recommend it."

Her friend looked at her warily. "Uh-huh."

The front door opened, letting in a blast of warm air. "Are we too late?"

Startled, Layla looked to where Mallory and Jack had just stormed into the place, looking a bit on the frazzled side. In fact, she noticed with some amount of satisfaction, she appeared to be the only one with her wits together on this fine Tuesday morning.

"What do you mean, are you too late?" Layla asked, eyeing Reilly, who was looking suspiciously guilty across from her. "Is someone dying?"

"What?" said Reilly, who was almost incapable of lying. "So I called them. What's the big deal?"

Layla shrugged, not even bothered by this. "It's not a big deal. It's just I'd like to know the reason why."

Mallory took one stool; Jack took the other. Mall reached for one of the sticky buns. "Anyone want this? No? Good," she said, without waiting for an answer. Around a mouthful of pastry, she said, "Reilly is worried about you. And, frankly, so am I."

Jack raised a hand as he appeared to look around

for something. "Add me to the list." He frowned. "Where's my coffee?"

Layla pushed her cup toward him as Reilly went to get more coffee for the latest additions.

Mall licked the sticky syrup off her lips. "I mean, no one, but no one, just up and quits a primo position like the one you had at the Center, Lay."

"No one?" She squared her shoulders. "Hmm. I kind of like knowing I'm setting a precedent."

"As what? The thousandth idiot to get involved with her boss then resign when it doesn't work out?"

Layla's mouth gaped open as she stared at her friend.

Jack glared at Mallory. "What she means is—"

Layla waved at him. "Mallory doesn't need an interpreter, Jack. She needs a roll of duct tape." She considered her brash friend. "Is that what you think? That I quit because Sam and I didn't work out?"

"Well…yeah," Mallory said in a flippant manner that made Layla laugh.

"You couldn't be further from the truth."

"So you and Sam aren't quitsville, then?" Reilly asked as she brought two more cups, a pot of coffee and another batch of sticky buns. Layla marveled at the ravenous way Mallory attacked the fare. You'd think she hadn't eaten in a week. She frowned as she realized that might be hitting too close to home.

"Well, what if I were to tell you that I've decided

I no longer want to be a professional general practitioner with my eye constantly on the bottom line?''

''I'd say you have student loans to think about.''

''And what if I responded by saying that they're
covered, that my job at the clinic is more than
enough to keep me living in the way I've grown
accustomed to, and that I've been thinking about
getting into producing documentaries?''

Reilly looked about ready to fall out of her chair,
Jack muttered something under his breath and went
off to get napkins, and Mallory stopped mid-chew,
looking a hairbreadth away from spitting the contents of her mouth into her coffee.

''What?'' Reilly and Mallory said at the same
time.

''You heard me correctly.'' Layla leaned her fore-
arms on the table and gazed steadily at her friends.

Mallory finally managed to swallow. ''I'd say you
were insane.''

''This thing with Sam,'' Reilly said, gesturing
blindly, ''it must be more serious than even we
knew. I mean…you've really gone off the deep
end.''

Mallory reached for a napkin Jack had put on the
table, fished a pen out of her purse and scribbled
something down. She pushed the napkin toward
Layla. ''That's the name of a good psychiatrist. I
did a piece on him a couple of months ago. He's on
the up and up.''

''I don't need a psychiatrist.'' Layla pushed the

napkin back. "There's nothing wrong with my mental faculties." She shrugged. "I just finally took a look at my bank book, that's all."

Her three friends stared at her.

"You know, my checks were being direct-deposited, and you know how I am about balancing stuff out. All I needed to know was that my loans were covered. And the remainder…" She grinned. "Well, after five years, the remainder is far more than I could have imagined."

Mallory shifted. "You looking to adopt? I'm up for grabs."

Layla laughed. "I've already adopted you, Mall. I've adopted all of you as my sisters and, of course, my brother."

Her friends continued to stare at her, Jack looking particularly wary and weary.

Layla drew in a deep breath. "Okay, I know you think this is about Sam. And, I guess, in a roundabout way it is. Only not in the way you'd believe."

Even Mallory had stopped her attack on the food. "Go on."

"Well," Layla said, running her finger round the rim of her cup. "He gave me some food for thought, that's all. Made me take a closer look at myself, my life." She shrugged. "And, well, I didn't like what I saw much."

"He dumped you?"

"Yes…no." She gestured vaguely with her hands. "It went both ways. But what he did do was point out a few things that I had buried so deep it had taken a shovel to uncover.''

''So you're getting back together?'' Reilly asked.

Layla was relieved when Mallory and Jack's gazes moved to Reilly instead.

''What? It's a valid question. I mean, if he helped rather than hurt her…''

Layla looked around the quaint little shop, so out of step with the rest of trendy L.A. It was a throwback to the past when *calories* was just a word in a dictionary, not a way of life. ''I never said he didn't hurt me.''

Mall snorted indelicately.

''But there's also no going back.'' She took a sip of coffee, finding it had cooled. She reached to warm it up with the pot Reilly had brought to the table, only to find Jack and Mall had already drained it. ''Anyway, I wouldn't even know how to.''

The bell above the door rang as a customer came in. Layla absently saw it was a woman maybe a decade older than her, well turned out, her clothes impeccably chosen, her short black hair coiffed. Layla noticed Reilly was watching her, just as the bell rang again and another woman entered. This one was younger than Layla in snug jeans, a cropped top and sporting a waist…what would you call that? Necklaces were for necks. So would that be a belly-lace? Or maybe a belly chain. Yes, that sounded better.

Reilly rolled her eyes to stare at the ceiling, her shoulders slumping.

Mallory took in the visitors as one of the counter girls attended to them. "That's not...?"

Reilly nodded, and Layla realized that the two women must be the wife and mistress she'd told her about the week before. "Every morning, just like clockwork." She lowered her voice. "They've even started sticking around instead of leaving with their orders, and they...they sit together."

"Oh, God," Layla and Mall said at the same time.

"Tell me about it."

Jack grimaced. "What are you guys talking about? No, wait." He held up a hand. "I don't want to know."

Reilly's shoulders came up and squared. "I can't deal with this any longer. It's long past time I did something."

"Did what?" Mallory asked.

"Introduced them," Reilly responded with a nod toward Layla.

"This, I gotta see," Mallory said, smiling over her cup.

They sat back and watched as Reilly did just as she promised.

But rather than paying attention to the reactions of the two women who were learning they shared the same man, Layla considered her friend. While Reilly had always been pretty, her self-esteem had not always been her greatest asset. Except she seemed to be doing much better in that department.

Layla smiled and looked down at her coffee. It seemed she wasn't the only one going through some radical changes....

16

MISERABLE. That's how Sam felt an entire month later as he stood under the thin rays of the Southern California autumn sun, the overwhelming scent of flowers making him think of funerals rather than weddings. He tugged at the collar of his shirt, reminding himself that his mood was best kept to himself. His sister had already frowned at him over a half a dozen times since he'd arrived at the wedding location. The location being a tiny patch of land out in the middle of nowhere between San Bernardino and Barstow where his sister lived with her deadbeat boyfriend in what was little more than a shack of a house.

It was a good thing his parents hadn't been able to make it, he thought. Forget that the bride didn't care if she was seen in her simple dress before the ceremony. She had her arm linked with Brian's as they greeted the twenty-five or so guests who had shown up for the funeral…er, event. Then again, since the two had been living together for the past two years, there probably wasn't much point in adhering to tradition. Besides, bad luck had entered his sister's life the moment Brian had.

"If you grind your teeth any harder you won't have any left to eat with," Heather said, coming to stand next to him near the garage, a one-car structure that was nearly as big as the house.

Sam made an effort to smile, gave up, then glanced at his watch. "When is this thing supposed to get under way?"

Heather smiled at him, her pretty face unperturbed. "We're waiting for one last guest."

"Ah," he said as if that explained everything, when, in fact, it hadn't answered his question.

He looked at where Brian already held a can of beer, and Sam's back teeth shuddered.

The sound of a car's tires spitting gravel sounded behind him.

"And there she is now," Heather said.

Sam turned idly, expecting to see one of his sister's tie-dye set. Instead he watched Layla climb out of her old Pontiac, looking fresh and sexy and altogether mouthwatering in a light-green dress.

Now his sister's comment about waiting for someone made perfect sense.

"Am I late?" Layla asked, seeming to go out of her way to look everywhere but into his eyes.

Heather took her hands in hers. "No. You're right on time." She pulled her toward the other guests. "Come on. Let me introduce you around."

Finally Layla's eyes met his. Sam couldn't seem to force a swallow through his throat as his gaze remained glued to hers while she passed. What was she doing here? And, more importantly, what was he going to do about it?

A month had passed since he'd left her sitting in her car in that trailer park. Four weeks since she'd resigned without so much as an explanation. Twenty-eight tortured nights and even harder days in which he alternately hated himself for saying what he had, missed her like hell and tried to pretend that he didn't care one way or another about her.

But seeing her now...

He tugged at his collar again.

Seeing her now made him want to touch her. As if through the simple action of doing so he could once again find his center, his core, his foundation.

"I need a drink," he muttered to no one in particular and made his way to the shaky card table set up in the shade of the boxy house. He stuck his hand in a large bucketful of bottles and cans and ice, pulled out a soda, then went back in until he got a beer. He popped the top and began to pour it down his parched throat.

"Your sister's nice." The familiar voice next to him made his entire body tighten.

He turned into the sun and squinted at the woman who had shown him what love was—completely by accident because she'd proven that she didn't know how to love.

"My sister's an idiot."

Layla smiled. "Still haven't reconciled with the groom, I see."

"You see correctly." At least in this case. "What, are you and my sister best friends now?"

Layla blanched at the barbed remark then looked down to where she kept smoothing the linen of her dress over her slender hips. "Actually this is the first time we've met face-to-face." She warily met his eyes. "I told you I would come. So I'm here."

"Nancy. My assistant is behind this, isn't she? She put you in touch with Heather?"

He knew from Layla's expression that was the case. "Only Nancy didn't call me. I called her. The rest…"

The rest he could guess.

He didn't know what bothered him more. That she'd been in touch with his secretary talking about his sister without his knowing, or that his secretary had given her his sister's number. Then there was Heather herself playing the indirect role of matchmaker when she couldn't even choose a decent match for herself.

"She looks beautiful, doesn't she?" Layla said quietly.

Sam was surprised by the words. He blinked to find Layla looking at his sister. And for the first time since he and Heather had gone for that walk on the pier, since she'd told him of her intentions to marry, he saw her. Just simply saw her. His sister. Little Heather with her nearly white-blond hair, her genuine smile, her gentle nature. As he took her in, noted how beautiful she looked, his muscles slowly began to relax.

Yes. He realized Layla was right. Heather did look beautiful.

She also looked so completely happy that his heart ached.

"You can't choose who you love, Sam."

His sister's words echoed through his mind. And he realized something else. That this day wasn't about Brian. Wasn't about the suitability of the groom or what might happen in the future. It was about now, today. And it was completely about his sister and her happiness.

A thick ball of emotion formed in his throat. He slowly shifted his gaze to take in the woman who had put the lump there.

Layla.

As he watched her gazing at Heather, something else grabbed his heart. A sense of gratitude so great that he was paralyzed on the spot. He felt a kind of connection that nearly overwhelmed him with its strength.

Oh, he'd seen this kind of connection in other people. In his parents. In others' marriages. But he hadn't really identified it until now. Until with one direct statement Layla had managed to point out all that really mattered. And she had diffused a situation that had the potential to ruin everyone's day.

His sister was in love and this was what she wanted. That's really where it began and ended, wasn't it?

He finally managed to swallow, remembering that Layla had told him, when she'd first offered to come with him to the wedding, that she had ways of helping him through this. Before he'd uttered those fateful words. Before she'd told him it was over and he'd come to think that it was, too. He'd thought her assistance would be somehow sexual. Something to distract him.

Instead she'd helped him to see the truth.

Layla slowly turned and met his gaze head-on. In her eyes he saw the knowing, the understanding, and, yes, even the passion that no amount of sex would be able to completely erase. And he saw the love that he'd been afraid she didn't feel. Saw the love in the depths of her green eyes that he also felt, with his entire being.

"Are you ready?" Heather asked, coming to stand in front of him.

Sam blinked, tearing his gaze from Layla and taking in his sister. In the background a long-haired guy with a guitar began strumming a simple tune.

He smiled, then reached for Heather's hands. In her face, he read surprise. Then gratitude. Then a joy so great it nearly did him in.

Sam affectionately kissed her cheek then tucked her hand into the crook of his arm. "Let's go give you away to the man you love."

AT LEAST someone was getting a happily-ever-after ending, Layla thought later that night. She finished gathering together snacks in her tiny kitchen and carried them out into the living room where Mallory, Reilly and Jack were sitting around the coffee table embroiled in their latest discussion. Which right now happened to be cigarette smoking in public places.

"It smells," Reilly said, wrinkling her nose.

"Reilly, hon, it kills," Mallory said.

Jack got up from his chair. "The fumes you inhale on the Santa Monica freeway during rush hour will kill you faster than being in a room with smokers for the rest of your life," he grumbled. "I'm going outside."

Layla put down the bowls and snacks then sat down on the sofa. "I thought he quit."

Mallory immediately dug in, pouring a bag of corn chips into a bowl then crunching down on three at a time. "He cut back." She reached for her cola. "Next time we do this at my place."

Reilly and Layla shared a glance. Every now and again Mallory threw the suggestion out, and her friends used every trick in the book to keep from going to her apartment.

"So," Layla said, focusing instead on Reilly, "what's the latest on the wife-mistress thing?"

Reilly shrugged as she crossed her legs, her diet soda clutched in her hands. Layla recognized the move. As long as Reilly was holding something, she couldn't reach for something else. Namely food. "They're no longer doing the same man."

"Are they both still alive?" Mallory asked. "I mean, when you got up at the shop and told them who they both were...well, even I almost dove for cover."

Reilly smiled. "Interestingly enough, they both

dumped the pig and kept the friendship. The wife is actually staying with the mistress until she finds her own place and they both come into the shop together every morning, sit at the same table and seem closer than ever.''

Mallory stopped mid-chew. ''You're kidding me?''

''Nope.''

''Another happy ending,'' Layla sighed.

Reilly smiled. ''Well, except for the husband.''

''Husband-slash-cheating bastard,'' Mallory pointed out.

''Then there's that.''

''Anyway, forget all that,'' Mall said. ''I want to know how the wedding went.''

''Wedding?'' Reilly asked.

Mall chewed the chips in her mouth then swallowed. ''Today Layla went to Sam's sister's wedding.''

Reilly's hazel eyes grew as large as the bottom of her soda can. ''I thought you weren't seeing him anymore.''

''I'm not.'' Layla cleared her throat and pretended an interest in the junk food covering the table.

Reilly was clearly confused. ''Then how can you go to his sister's wedding?''

''Because I was invited.'' Layla made a face as she settled on one of the sticky buns from Sugar 'n' Spice that Reilly had contributed. ''Well, actually, I wasn't invited. I kind of invited myself. You see, I promised Sam I would go with him—he was having a really hard time accepting his sister's fiancé—you know, before we split, and, well, a promise is a promise.'' She smiled fondly as she dragged her finger along the syrup-covered top of the pastry. ''And despite how difficult it was to see him again, it was nice that Sam finally appeared to accept that it wasn't his sister's husband that mattered, but his sister herself.''

She stuck her finger into her mouth and moaned in appreciation, thinking she could die right then and there and not want for anything else.

Well, aside from Sam.

''He didn't try to talk to you?'' Reilly asked.

''We talked,'' Layla grudgingly admitted. But precious little. The ceremony had started pretty much the minute she'd arrived. And afterward…well, afterward, what with the cake-cutting and the reception, there hadn't been much opportunity to talk to Sam again.

She shrugged. ''I guess if I needed proof that it was over…well, today was it.''

''Moron,'' Mallory said.

''Idiot,'' Reilly agreed.

''Who?'' Layla asked. ''Him or me?''

''Him, of course.'' Mallory opened another bag of snacks and poured them into a bowl at the same time that she picked a corner off a sticky bun.

They heard male laughter from the hallway and the three of them fell silent.

Certainly Jack wasn't laughing by himself at something they'd said?

"Actually, I'm coming to see that I'm the bigger fool," Layla said quietly. "Sam...Sam is Dr. Lovejoy." She shivered and smiled instead of trying to stop the reaction. "And..."

And what? How could she express this? She briefly bit her bottom lip.

"And I forgot that aside from the infamous Dr. Lovejoy persona...well, he is also a man. A man who made me laugh. Who gave me more orgasms in one week than I'd had in my entire adult life, with or without a vib—"

"'Nough said." Mallory held up her hand.

Male voices and again laughter from the hall.

That was odd....

The door opened, letting Jack in along with the smell of cigarette smoke. "We have a visitor," he said.

A visitor? But...

Then, just like that, Sam's tall, broad, handsome frame was filling the doorway, looking better than any sweet Reilly's shop had to offer up.

"Poker, anyone?" he asked, although his gaze appeared to say so much more as it locked onto Layla's.

AN HOUR later, Layla's hands shook as she busied herself straightening up the living room. She still couldn't believe Sam had come. Couldn't believe he was still there. And while her friends initially had stuck around, had even tried to scare up that game of poker Sam suggested, it was plain that both she and Sam weren't really a part of the group. Layla couldn't stop looking at him, and, it seemed, Sam couldn't stop looking at her. She would begin a sentence, then halfway through completely lose her train of thought. Sam would try to crack a joke and completely flub up the punch line. And while her friends had kept up a pretty steady chatter, she couldn't for the life of her remember what any of them had said.

Ultimately, it had been Jack who had ushered Mallory and Reilly out with the promise of ice cream when the two other women had seemed content to sit there and watch things unfold.

And now Layla didn't know what to say. If, indeed, she was even capable of speech. She wasn't all that convinced she was. After all, neither of them had said anything for the past ten minutes while Sam had helped her put away chips and dip, and pile soda cans into the recycling bin.

"Layla?"

Finally a word broke the silence. She released a breath, instantly relieved.

"Sam, I—"

She turned and found him standing directly behind her in the kitchen. "Shh," he said, putting a finger to her lips, his mesmerizing brown eyes fathomless as she stared into them. "There's something I need to tell you before you share what you want to say. Is that okay?"

Spellbound, Layla could only nod.

He dropped the finger he'd pressed to her lips, his

gaze seemingly glued there, on her mouth. She licked her lips, wondering if she'd ever felt more nervous in her life.

"I wanted to tell you how very wrong I was," he said, so quietly she nearly didn't hear him.

Layla's heart skipped a beat as her brain tried to process his words. But seeing as she'd come to view so much truth in what he'd told her a month ago, she couldn't seem to accept what he was saying now.

"I don't understand…" she whispered.

A grin began to crease the sides of his mouth, then disappeared just as quickly. "It was wrong of me to have said what I did in the way I said it," he explained. He reached out and tucked behind her ear a strand of hair that had escaped her ponytail. "My mother was always fond of the saying 'if you can't say something nice, don't say anything at all.' While I disagreed with her philosophy, it's one I always tried to live by." He searched her eyes as if looking for something. "Then last month…" He drifted off. "Last month I unleashed a part of me on you that…well, that surprised even me."

From the other room came the low sounds of David Koz's saxophone. The music combined with the feel of Sam's fingers lingering on her neck made Layla's pulse kick up.

"And, honestly, I didn't know how to handle what came out."

Layla dropped her gaze to his chest.

"Then there was today."

The tone of his voice pulled her gaze back up. In his face she saw such an expression of wonder, of awe, that just looking at him took her breath away.

"I don't know. After what happened between us last month, I thought it was over. Then I saw you and..." He paused for several moments.

And what? her heart quietly cried.

"And I felt like a hole I hadn't known existed had been filled again. Not only filled, but filled to overflowing. Just looking at you. Then you did what you did..."

Layla swallowed hard, the quiet click sounding loud in the kitchen. "I didn't do anything."

His smile melted into a grin. "Oh, yes, you did. You gave me my sister back."

His fingers traveled over her shoulder, down her arm, then gripped her hand, bringing it to his chest. He flattened her palm over his heart.

"And you showed me what lay inside here."

Layla's eyes welled to the point that he became a blur.

He kissed her hand then held it tightly between them. "Another thing I was wrong about was your capacity for love. I made the mistake of thinking that if a person didn't verbally express it, well, it didn't exist. But with one look into your face, one glimpse into your eyes this morning, I felt love so powerfully that it nearly knocked me over."

Layla dropped her chin to her chest and tried to blink back her tears before she turned into a blubbering idiot.

"And I knew that you were the one," he murmured. "I knew you were that one person in this world that I could say anything to without the fear of losing you. I knew that you were the one person who knew me better than even I knew myself. I knew that you were the one person I could trust with my heart. Totally. Completely. With absolutely no reservations."

He quietly cleared his throat. "Will you marry me, Layla?"

She stared at him as if he'd gone mad. "Wh...what?"

She might not have been able to see him all that well, but she was pretty sure her hearing was still working correctly. And unless she was mistaken, he had just asked her to become his wife.

"Oh, I think you heard me," he said, leaning forward and kissing the tip of her nose, then brushing his lips against hers. "But I'll say it again. I'll say it until your answer is yes. Marry me, Layla."

"Oh, God," she whispered, covering her face with her hands.

The sound of her ragged breathing was all that filled the room for long minutes. Enough time for the CD playing in the other room to switch tracks. And long enough for Layla to realize that she wasn't caught in some parallel universe.

"You don't have to answer me now," Sam said.

Layla slowly managed to regain control of her sight even though her heart felt as though it might pound straight out of her chest. "Are you done talking yet?"

He blinked at her, clearly surprised.

She smiled. "You do that a lot, you know." She moved her hand like a puppet. "Talk, talk, talk. I swear, I bet your mother used to threaten to stick a sock in that trap of yours."

He didn't appear to know how to react, then finally he chuckled.

"Because if you are done, I have a few things of my own to say."

The grin faded from his face.

"What you said—about your being wrong—you are so wrong." She flapped her hand in the air. "What I mean is, what you said that day in the car, everything you said, was right on target. I...I was looking for an excuse to shut you out. Grasping onto anything, everything I could to stop us, you and me, from going any further." She tucked her own hair behind her ear. "You..." She searched his face. "Well, frankly, Sam Lovejoy, you scare the hell out of me."

She took a deep breath, noticing the way his mouth began turning up in a smile.

"Without my even being aware of it, you stole into my life and made away with my heart before I could even blink." She shook her head with wonder. "I'd spent so much of my life thinking, believing that I was the one in control, that I was in charge of my own destiny. Even the thought that I wasn't, that somehow you had taken away a bit of that control, well…I couldn't let that happen.''

She tilted her head to the side, taking in every gorgeous inch of his face.

''But I couldn't even control that, could I? Because no matter if we're together or apart…well, you have that control, don't you?''

Sam slid his hands across either side of her neck. ''Oh, Lay, I don't think it's a matter of one or the other of us having control. I think that together…well, together the entire dynamic changes. We're no longer you or me…we're us.''

She eyed his mouth, mere millimeters away from hers, a sob nearly choking off her ability to speak. ''Oh, God, you're right.'' She rested her forehead against his chin. ''Doesn't that frighten you just a little bit?''

His voice lowered to a whisper. ''It terrifies me.''

Layla smiled and rested her cheek against the hard wall of his chest. For long moments she did nothing but listen to the unsteady beat of his heart and think about how she was putting her heart at great risk. Then she said, simply, ''Yes.'' She sniffed and pulled back so she could look at him as she spoke. ''Yes, Dr. Sam Lovejoy, I'll marry you.''

He stared at her for a long moment, then leaned in to kiss her. What started slow and sweet quickly escalated to fierce and hungry, until Sam pulled away, leaving them both out of breath.

''Jesus,'' he murmured, cupping the back of her head with his hand and pressing her back to his chest. "Waiting until the wedding is going to be the hardest thing I've ever done."

Layla's eyes opened wide. "What?"

"Waiting until the wedding, you know, to make love, is going to be pure torture."

She jerked away from his touch only to find him grinning at her in wicked wonder.

"Gotcha," he murmured.

Layla worked her fingers up the hem of his T-shirt then kissed him deeply. "No, Sam, I think we both have each other."

*   *   *   *   *

*Don't miss Reilly's story, FLAVOR OF THE
MONTH, which blazes its way into
bookstores next month…*